215

MORTAL TASTE

Recent Titles by J M Gregson from Severn House

Lambert and Hook Mysteries

AN ACADEMIC DEATH
DEATH ON THE ELEVENTH HOLE
GIRL GONE MISSING
MORTAL TASTE
AN UNSUITABLE DEATH

Detective Inspector Peach Mysteries

TO KILL A WIFE
THE LANCASHIRE LEOPARD
A LITTLE LEARNING
MISSING, PRESUMED DEAD
MURDER AT THE LODGE
A TURBULENT PRIEST
WHO SAW HIM DIE?

MORTAL TASTE

J.M. Gregson

This first world edition published in Great Britain 2003 by
SEVERN HOUSE PUBLISHERS LTD of
9–15 High Street, Sutton, Surrey SM1 1DF.
This first world edition published in the USA 2003 by
SEVERN HOUSE PUBLISHERS INC of
595 Madison Avenue, New York, N.Y. 10022.

British Library Cataloguing in Publication Data

Gregson, J. M. (James Michael)
    Mortal taste
    1. Lambert, Superintendent John (Fictitious character) - Fiction
    2. Hook, Sergeant Bert (Fictitious character) - Fiction
    3. Police - England - Gloucestershire - Fiction
    4. Cheltenham (England) - Fiction
    5. Detective and mystery stories
    I. Title
    823.9'14 [F]

    ISBN 0-7278-5989-7

Typeset by Palimpsest Book Production Ltd.,
Polmont, Stirlingshire, Scotland.
Printed and bound in Great Britain by
MPG Books Ltd., Bodmin, Cornwall.

To Peter Landau and David Every –
two very successful head teachers, who are otherwise
quite unlike the one in this book!

Of man's first disobedience, and the fruit
Of that forbidden tree, whose mortal taste
Brought death into the world, and all our woe,
With loss of Eden . . .

John Milton, *Paradise Lost*

One

C heltenham is one of the finest spa towns in Europe. It has a wealth of Regency terraces lining elegant squares, crescents and open spaces. George III, that inveterate frequenter of spas, visited the town in 1788 and set his seal of approval upon it.

It is not at all the sort of place you would identify with violent death.

For the British, the name of Cheltenham conjures up echoes of the Empire in retirement. It was when military officers and colonial administrators returning from the tropics discovered the beneficial effects of the mineral waters that the elegant new town was established. Between 1800 and 1840, the discernment and good taste of people steeped in a classical culture achieved its architectural fulfilment amidst the wide streets and tree-shaded open spaces of the new town.

This has always been a place for civilized debate, not an arena for the knife and the bullet.

Yet there is another Cheltenham beyond the Regency ironwork balconies and verandas, beyond the elegance of Lansdown Place and Montpellier Walk. The ubiquitous motor car has made its inevitable and relentless impact. The town is intersected by the A40 and five radiating major routes, so that it is now one of the most frustrating places in which to drive and one of the most difficult in which to park.

Perhaps it is better communications which have brought some very undesirable people into this cultivated town.

Yet road and rail have brought new sources of employment

to an ancient part of England. The town is one of the few in the country where manufacturing industry, varying from thermostatic valves to watches and clocks, is thriving in the new century. Its festivals of music and literature bring creative forces into the town, but Cheltenham is probably more famous for the racecourse on its northern side, which brings an influx of visitors, most but not all of them welcome, into the ancient spa town.

The educational facilities of the town reflect similar contrasts and tensions between tradition and modernity. On the Bath Road are two schools which enjoy a national fame. The Cheltenham College for Boys, built between 1841 and 1843 in early Gothic Revival style, thrived as a public school for the sons of Indian Army officers. Nearby is the Cheltenham Ladies' College, founded by Miss Beale, an ardent Victorian champion of good education for girls, a school now renowned and caricatured throughout the country as the emblem of Establishment good taste and breeding.

In other and newer parts of the town, among the harsher brick buildings of the second half of the twentieth century, there are other schools, educating the children of the workers and the unemployed of a modern industrial complex. Greenwood Comprehensive has very different buildings and a very different ethos from those of Cheltenham Ladies' College and the Cheltenham College for Boys.

Greenwood has equal numbers of boys and girls, for a start, and a much wider range of the social classes among its parents. It also has a far greater proportion of single parents attending – or failing to attend – its regular parents' evenings, where the educational progress of its clientele is discussed. And as might be expected, this school has its share of what the jargon of the day calls social problems. Drugs have exchanged hands outside its gates, especially in the convenient darkness of winter evenings.

Nevertheless, education is not the environment in which you would expect a man to have his head blown away.

Greenwood Comprehensive School's sixth form enjoys an interesting range of distinguished visitors, summoned to offer their experience and their views of life to those about to enter its full challenges. But policemen and social workers are also frequent visitors to the school, and two representatives of that burgeoning profession of the twenty-first century – the counsellor – are busily employed within the school.

Yet let no one convince you that good education cannot be provided in establishments like Greenwood Comprehensive. There are bad schools working among the problems thrown up by settings like this, some of them almost defeated by the difficulties of staffing and resources. But there are also some very good schools, providing a lively and stimulating environment for learning amongst the social problems which surround them.

Greenwood Comprehensive was one of these at the time of these events. It came agreeably high in the league tables of schools by which a desperate government tried to raise standards. If a proper allowance had been made for the background of its intake and the problems of its environment, it might well have come in the very top sections of the tables. The two famous private schools a few miles away had pupil-teacher ratios which were half those of Greenwood.

But Greenwood Comprehensive School was the very last place where you would expect murder to be stalking.

Every good school has a good head teacher. Because of the way the state system is set up, because of the power of the head to set the spirit and standards of the school, it is almost impossible to have a highly effective school without a highly effective head. Greenwood was no exception to this rule.

Peter Logan had been its head teacher for five years. By a combination of vision, foresight and energy, he had made it one of the best schools of its kind in Gloucestershire. Energy might seem a mundane quality to outsiders, but it was the most important of these three in the day-to-day efficiency of a large school, and Peter had energy in abundance.

Yet one would have said that Peter Logan was not at all the kind of person who would get himself involved in murder.

For the energy which drove him was the servant of an unswerving vision. In Logan's view, his school was already the best in the county. In a few years, it would be one of the best in the country. There were two key appointments coming up in the next few months, a Deputy Head and a Head of Sixth Form Studies. Peter knew what he wanted, and would make sure that he got it. Even if the first set of interviews didn't produce the right person, he would wait and re-advertise. Staff appointments were the most important decisions you ever made in a school, and it was worth putting up with short-term inconvenience to get the right person.

All this Peter Logan knew too well for it to need repetition. He was enunciating it for the benefit of his governors at their meeting on this Monday evening. They were a good body of citizens, on the whole. They wanted the school to succeed and took notice of what the Head told them. Once he had reassured them, they were only too eager to help its Head to implement his policies. They were backing a good man, after all. Peter had already convinced them of that: year by year, he brought them solid evidence of success in the school's examination results.

Everyone says that exam performance should not be the sole measure of a school's success, that education is about more intangible things than merely passing exams and taking the first successful steps in life's rat race. And everyone promptly adopts exam results as the only reliable guide to a school's progress.

But that was all right. The state school came out very well on the GCSE and A-level counts. Greenwood and Peter Logan produced the goods, and the school went forward, and everyone was happy.

Or almost everyone. One person in the governors' meeting watched the head teacher steadily, with no evidence of emotion. One person listened not to the arguments he outlined but to the ambition which lay behind them. One person weighed everything Peter Logan said and found it wanting. It was not objective, but one person was not concerned with being objective about the man who led Greenwood Comprehensive.

One governor at least was consumed with a surprising hatred of this popular head teacher.

The meeting proceeded smoothly enough. Peter Logan announced that the new bank of computers had been installed in the school's IT centre. There were mutters of pleasure all round the table, even from the three elderly local councillors, who had no acquaintance with computers. Technology was always impressive, especially when you did not understand it.

Various sponsorships had been arranged with local industry, which would not only defray educational costs for hard-pressed taxpayers but also establish employment links for the future. The governors nodded sagely: schools must not be ivory towers.

This meeting, on the twenty-first of September, was the first one of the new academic year, so Peter Logan gave a simplified summary of the summer examination results and the final count of the number of pupils entering higher education, which had climbed over a hundred for the first time. He smiled with modest confidence at the earnest faces round the big table, and almost provoked a round of applause.

The Chairman of the Governors thanked the Head for his lucid account of past successes and future plans. The meeting broke up in a quiet aura of self-congratulation: it is always more pleasant to be involved in a winning enterprise, to be agreeably swept along in the momentum of success.

Tea and biscuits were brought in at the end of the meeting. The buzz of conversation and informal exchange of ideas sounded almost muted at one end of a school hall which could accommodate a thousand pupils. Inevitably, Peter Logan's voice sounded continually above the rest; he was constantly asked for information, and his genuine enthusiasm for present achievement and future potential encouraged him to hold forth at length about his school.

His Chairman of Governors announced eventually that he must be away, and most of his colleagues on the governing body drifted off in his wake. Peter Logan thanked them individually as they left, then retired to his own room for a brief period of silence and recuperation. Even a naturally gregarious man needed time alone. Even a man as much at home with his destiny as the successful head of a big school found some strain in meetings such as the one which had just gone so successfully. And there were preparations to make for the next school day, which would begin in another eleven hours.

Logan's was the last car to leave the car park. He walked out serenely to it in the warm darkness of early autumn, sniffing the air appreciatively in unaccustomed isolation. Usually there was the sound of childish voices all around this part of the school. He eased his Rover 75 past the caretaker's house and drove unhurriedly and contentedly through the school gates and into the wider world outside the one he controlled.

He did not see the other car which came from beneath the trees of the cul de sac near the school gates. It followed him at a discreet distance when he turned on to the main road, its attendance marked by no more than the twin beams of dipped headlights, a good eighty yards behind him.

The last thing Peter Logan was thinking about was murder.

Two

They met on Mondays. Each of them felt a little easier arriving at the house in autumn, as the evenings drew in and night came earlier. You did not want to be seen attending such gatherings in the daylight. Next month, at the end of October, the hour would have gone back, and they would bring the times of their meetings forward. Somehow winter seemed to most of them the most appropriate season for these exchanges.

All of them were men, and one or two of them looked seedy as well as shifty as they arrived. These were the kind of people you would look back at when you had passed them, to check that they were not up to something; they had a naturally furtive air about them, and behaved as if they had long since recognized the impossibility of appearing respectable. They wore clothes which were not just shabby but dirty as well, and their hair was lank and unkempt.

But these few were the exception. For the most part, the members of the group who assembled at the semi-detached house in the quiet suburbs of Cheltenham were dressed neatly, even expensively, and both their clothes and their bearing were respectable to the point of anonymity. This was an activity where you cultivated anonymity, as the best defence against discovery.

None of them stood for long at the door of the house. Not one of them rang the bell and waited for admission. The door was not quite closed, and each of them as they arrived pushed at its paint-blistered surface and moved softly inside, before carefully restoring the door to its previous position, ready for the next quiet entry. Low-key movement and an awareness of the need to frustrate the curious world around them came naturally to each member of this group. When you were breaking the law, it behoved everyone to be careful.

Inside the house, with the protection of solid walls about them, people gradually became more relaxed. The conversation flowed a little more easily as the cheap wine encouraged it. But the atmosphere was never lively, and the decibel level never rose above a quiet hum. Even as they sipped the wine and talked to their fellows, many of the men who met like this felt an unvoiced contempt for their companions. It was an emotion which was only surpassed by the deeper contempt they felt for themselves.

Not all of them, however. Some of them had gone beyond that stage to something more reckless, a defiant proclamation of their strangeness which brought them near to something like elation.

These were the men who produced the video cassettes and outlined their contents with pride and excitement. There was a heavy silence, then a tense, suppressed animation among the group as the videos were slipped into the player. Then came a sigh of collective satisfaction as the wide eyes of the children looked at the camera and the entertainment began.

None of the men looked at each other as the showing proceeded. The sounds in the dimly lit room were confined to the occasional involuntary groan of pleasure.

Even when the single light in the middle of the room went on at the end of the showings, there was not much conversation. This was a diverse group of men; they had little in common except their perversion, and words did not flow easily from many of them.

There was one exception, however. The man who had watched the videos from the corner of the room was articulate enough, when he chose to be. But that was in contexts other than this. He was a good conversationalist in these other settings. In the rest of his life, he liked to think of himself as completely normal: doing the conventional thing was becoming more and more important to him in that other, public section of his existence. It was almost as if he could compensate for his membership of this group by being excessively normal in other areas.

He was an intelligent man, so he did not disguise from himself that this dark interest of his was – well, illegal. At one time, he might have said sinful, but he had long since forsaken the concept of sin.

He bought copies of two of the video cassettes to take away with him. And he left the house as soon as he could, once he had got what he wanted. Later, in the privacy of his own room, he would feel the now-familiar disgust with himself and what he was about. For the moment, his distaste extended only to the excited men around him. In truth, he found his fellows at this gathering a sorry crew and was happy enough to leave their company quickly.

He looked carefully to left and right from the darkened drive of the house before he went swiftly to his car. You couldn't be too careful, with video cassettes like these in your briefcase. And he felt he had more to lose than the rest of the men he had left behind him.

When a schoolteacher was a paedophile, he had to be very careful indeed.

'How did the governors' meeting go?'

Jane Logan threw him the question as soon as he came into the sitting room. Might as well get it over with.

Her husband did not treat it as a conventional enquiry. 'Well enough. They were interested to hear about the numbers going to university and our plans for the future. They'll support me in the scheme for the new library and information centre, I think. Mind you, I haven't told them how much it's going to cost yet!' That small, unconscious grin came to Peter

Logan's lips, the one he had when he anticipated a challenge. The one she had once found so attractive.

'Have you eaten?'

'Yes. I sent out for a pizza from the shop near the school.'

She might have ribbed him once about fast food and the example he set to his pupils. Instead, she said, 'I'll get us a drink, then,' and went into the kitchen. She was shocked by her own feelings. She hadn't seen Peter for fourteen hours, yet already she wanted to be away from him.

She knew he was studying her over the top of his paper when she took the tray with its teapot and cups back into the room. 'You've kept your looks, Jane,' he said, as if he was noticing it for the first time. He sounded slightly surprised, and rather spoiled the effect of the compliment by following up with the observation: 'They say that's especially difficult for blonde, blue-eyed types like you, but my wife seems to have managed it.'

'Whereas you have just got yourself more and more important jobs. Working on the theory that power is the great aphrodisiac, I suppose.'

'Haven't noticed it working that way recently. Not where you're concerned, that is.' He was behind the pages of the *Guardian*, studiously avoiding any eye contact, trying to cloak a serious observation as a throwaway remark. He had always done that; she realized now that she hated it.

'Perhaps you should pay a little more attention to your wife and a little less attention to the job.' She said it tartly, more bitchily than she intended, and answered his retreat behind the paper by returning to the book she had been reading when he arrived. He had turned off the Schubert CD she had been listening to and put on the television. It flickered inconsequentially in the corner of the room, with neither of them watching or listening to it.

To her surprise, he took her comment seriously. 'You're right, darling, I have been neglecting you. Now that I'm in the job I wanted, you deserve much more attention.' She noted his priorities with a wry smile, but didn't speak. She had never used the term 'darling' to him; it seemed to drop falsely from his lips now, where once she had accepted it.

He waited for the reaction which did not come from her, and then said, 'It's always busy at the beginning of a new school year, but I must find time for you now that everything is under way. Perhaps we should book a weekend away. A long weekend, at half-term, perhaps?'

That was the very last thing she wanted. She felt her heart thumping as she said, 'There's no need for that, really. I quite understand that you're very busy at school.'

It came out as though delivered by an understanding stranger, but he did not seem to notice. 'No, I've been neglecting you. I must do something about that, or someone else will step in. Pretty women like you shouldn't be neglected!' He grinned at her over his teacup, then raised it in a mock toast to her beauty. She looked steadily back at him, putting on the poker face she had cultivated over these past few weeks, concealing what she really felt about him, forcing herself eventually into a small, answering smile.

He was easily enough deceived, but that had its consequences. Twenty minutes later, as she undressed, he ran his fingers down her spine, took her roughly into his arms, insisted on making love to her.

The familiar hands in the familiar bed were like a stranger's upon her, but without the excitement that strangeness should have brought. He was rough in his love-making, and she tried to give him enough response to allay any suspicions he might have had. As he came noisily, she arched her back and simulated an orgasm of her own, her low moans lost in the ecstasy of his pleasure.

It worked well enough, apparently, for when he fell back, Peter Logan breathed the words, 'That was good, Jane,' into her ear. And she felt the shame of her deception surge through her body, still rigid as her husband's went suddenly limp. He stroked the back of her neck a couple of times, the gesture he had always used to suggest that affection went beyond sex, and then fell heavily asleep.

Jane Logan lay awake on her back for a long time, staring at the invisible ceiling. She could not go on like this. She would have to do something about Peter, and quickly.

Three

S teve Fenton dressed rapidly. At least there was no problem getting into the bathroom these days, but the house
still felt curiously empty without Josie and the boys.

He didn't miss his wife and the rows they used to have:
the silence was a blessed relief from the blazing arguments
over trivialities which had dominated the last two years of
their marriage. But he still missed the boys; he stared glumly
at the empty table as he came into the kitchen and wondered
what they were doing at this minute.

He told himself he was avoiding the most tiresome aspects
of adolescence, that he still had a good relationship with
them, but he no longer attempted to disguise from himself
that he missed them, for all the teenage shrapnel which had
occasionally flashed around his ears. Perhaps he even missed
that: he had enjoyed fighting the war that was never a real
war with his sons, being gracious in his occasional victories,
regrouping after his small defeats.

He looked out down the narrow, trim rear garden as he
sat at the table with his bowl of cereals. At least he hadn't
let things go since the divorce, either at home or at work.
The house was clean and tidy and the garden was still full of
colour even at the end of September. It was in better condition
than ever, now that the boys and their ball games had gone,
he thought sadly. The busy Lizzies and dahlias might have
been looking a little blousy and jaded at the end of the
season, as if the first frost, which would cut them down,
might be something of a release, but given a mild autumn,

he'd be able to cut the odd perfectly shaped rose almost up to Christmas.

He grinned at himself: get yourself a life, Stephen Fenton. But he had always enjoyed making things grow, even when he'd been the age his own boys were now. And anyway, his own life was looking up, thank you. Things had taken a decided turn for the better since he'd got himself involved with—

The phone shrilled sharply, no more than three feet to his right, shattering his morning reverie with its insistence. A secretary's voice: 'Mr Fenton, I have Mr Weatherly for you. One moment, please.'

There was a click and a large, confident voice said, 'Steve, good morning to you. Hope I haven't got you out of bed too early.' A booming laugh at his own little joke.

Steve looked at his watch. It was still only twenty past eight but he said, 'I was just on my way out. I can be at the works within ten minutes from here.' He wondered why this man could still make him defensive, when he had his own business and was not accountable to anyone. The seventy-year-old Archie Weatherly was now a non-executive director of a national firm of building contractors, the one which had built the Gloucester link-up with the M5 which had eased congestion in this area.

Weatherly laughed at Steve's apologetic reaction; he was well used to it within his own hierarchy, and relished it when he met it outside the firm. He said, 'It's about the governors' meeting at Greenwood Comp. last night.'

Steve had known it would be. They never spoke about anything else. And yet Weatherly had specified Greenwood Comprehensive as if he needed to differentiate it from half a dozen other schools where he was a governor. Probably that came naturally to him; probably he was used to speaking in those terms about any enterprise in which he involved himself. Steve felt that he knew what was coming, but he said cautiously, 'It seemed to me to go quite well.'

14

'Well enough, I suppose. School's doing a good job, as far as I can tell.' His short laugh indicated that he could tell quite far. 'Surprisingly good, considering what those buggers are paid. I notice you didn't say anything last night.'

'There didn't seem to be much to say. The Head reported clearly enough on the present state of progress and answered the various queries without any hedging. I don't believe in speaking just for the sake of it.' That sounded a little barbed, as though he was getting at Weatherly, who had asked a couple of questions. Steve hadn't intended that effect, but he was suddenly quite pleased with himself.

'He's doing well, young Logan. We need to keep a tight rein on the bugger, though. We can't leave it to the old farts from the Council.'

Steve Fenton grinned. Archie Weatherly was speaking of local worthies who were perhaps five years younger than him. In terms of energy, though, he was probably right. 'I thought the meeting went well enough, as you said. If it ain't broke, don't fix it.'

'I've made a living by fixing things. I think you should take the chair again, Fenton.'

Steve wondered why he should find the use of his surname so irritating. It was probably no more than Weatherly's public school habit from long ago. He thrust aside the consideration of whether a man from such a background should be now attempting to control the future of a state school. 'I'm afraid I don't feel I can reverse my decision. Two years as Chairman was enough. My own business is expanding and I really haven't the time.' He wondered if that sounded as unconvincing to Weatherly as it did to him. 'In any case we couldn't just reverse things like that. The new Chair has certainly done nothing wrong, and—'

'There's no problem with that, Fenton. Just say the word and you'll be back in the chair at the next meeting.' As if he realized that sounded brutal, Weatherly added, 'You're the best man for the job, everyone knows that. You should never have stood down when you did.'

'I'm sorry. My decision is irreversible, I'm afraid.'

'You shouldn't say that.' Weatherly sounded piqued: he was not a man who was used to refusals. 'Just say you'll think about it and that will do for the moment.'

Having refused to concede the main point, Steve had enough of the shrewd businessman in his own make-up to refuse the compromise as well. 'I'm afraid I can't do that. As I explained at the time, I have two boys in the school myself. They'll be coming up to GCSEs in due course. I'm happy to be a parent-governor of the school, but being Chairman could put me in an embarrassing position if a conflict of interests arose.'

He was glad he had remembered that argument, however belatedly. As he had suspected, Weatherly did not really know enough about the state system and school governing bodies to argue the point in detail. The industrialist rumbled on for a few more sentences, but recognized that he could not dictate action to someone who was not on his pay-list. He eventually accepted failure with ill grace and rang off swiftly.

Steve Fenton glanced at his watch and left half his cup of tea behind. The bloody man had made him late for work, now. He might be the boss, but he liked to set the right example: it was a small-firm ethic which would have been completely foreign to Archie Weatherly.

But at least he hadn't given any hint of the real reason why he could no longer be Chairman of the Governors of Greenwood Comprehensive.

Peter Logan, the man Archie Weatherly was so anxious to control, was getting on with the business of running a large and busy school.

Weatherly remained an autocrat at heart, and delegation was not one of his several virtues. But Logan was very good at delegation. It was the only way to run a busy school

16

efficiently: you put the right people in place, and then you allocated the right jobs to them, swiftly and automatically. When two members of staff called in sick, the problem of covering their classes was passed automatically to the Senior Mistress, who dealt with timetabling and all its attendant problems. The School Secretary did not even have to refer the matter to the Head. And when the teachers who had lost their 'free' periods to cover their absent colleagues grumbled ritually in the staff room, it was not the Head who was the subject of their complaints.

Peter Logan dealt swiftly with the most urgent of the morning post and made a series of phone calls to follow up the decisions of last night's governors' meeting. There was no point in letting grass grow under your feet when jobs had to be done. He found his briskness and eagerness to despatch the problems of the day met a pleasing response in those around him, another sign that the school was running smoothly and productively.

By ten o'clock, he was sufficiently clear of the daily administrative trivia to walk around his school and take the pulse of its activities. He remembered one of his teaching colleagues in his first job saying of their head teacher, 'That bugger knows everything that goes on in this place!', his mock-frustration masking a real respect. Peter had always remembered that, had always tried to emulate the feat as a head. You couldn't know everything that was going on in a school of this size, but if you gave both the staff and the pupils the impression that you did, that could only improve the efficiency of the institution.

To those who might think he pried unnecessarily, he quoted one of his favourite maxims: 'Slack practice anywhere leads to slack teaching in the end!' he said sternly.

Teachers always respected you if you brought everything back to what happened in the classroom, to what was offered at what he still called 'the chalk-face', though chalk was rarely seen now in his school. If all the petty restrictions with which successive governments had surrounded and impeded his teachers resulted in more efficient teaching, then that was their only necessary justification, the yardstick against which everything should be measured. Peter believed that passionately, and his passion carried him through, even with those teachers who were irritated by his personality.

Logan slipped into a classroom to check on the progress of one of his probationary teachers, trying to allay her understandable nervousness by a reassuring smile from the back of the room. He made a note or two to give her later in the day: she would be fine, once she gathered a little more experience.

He caught one of the old hands in the geography department enjoying a quiet and highly illicit smoke in the maps room, and allowed himself a secret smile only when he was well out of the discomfited man's vision. He reminded a PE teacher that the less able among his classes needed at least as much of his attention as the gifted gymnasts, especially now, when research about overweight and unfit children was dominating the media.

There was scope here for a press article about the attention his school was giving to this problem; he made a note to put his newly appointed media liaison officer – an enthusiastic young English teacher who saw himself as a journalist manqué – in touch with the PE department, to prepare a release for the local paper.

The representatives of the local press, radio and television could be useful allies. Most of his head teacher colleagues in other schools gave them nothing other than a tight-lipped 'No comment' and thus got only negative publicity. Yet these people could be helpful enough, if you handled them right: you needed to give them a ready-made story. Give them easy copy and they wouldn't ask you embarrassing questions. Serve them up a good story about the school's PE policy and a few quotes from slim, bright-eyed children and they'd produce a positive article about the way the school was tackling a national problem. Refuse to co-operate and you'd find them photographing fat kids at the gates and getting negative quotes to turn into headlines.

Peter had a cup of coffee in the crowded staff-room during morning break and managed brief exchanges with three of his heads of subject departments. Once this was done, he even had time to chat about the opening of the soccer season, and the erratic early progress of Cheltenham United in the second division of the Football League.

Yet not all was sweetness and light in this progressive school. A troubled young teacher took him to one side to report on two incidences of bullying in the third year. He had insisted that he wanted to know immediately about bullying, whether physical or mental. It was inevitable with over a thousand children in the school that they would have instances of this modern evil, but he wanted them investigated thoroughly and eliminated at source. A happy child is a learning child, and vice versa: it was a Logan maxim that had been elevated into a cliché over the years, but none the less true for that.

It was not until the bells rang for the end of morning school that Peter was prepared to indulge a more private pleasure. A man with a passion to make his school the best is not immune from other, more selfish and individual emotions. A man has his needs, and Logan found that his sexual drive was heightened by his professional successes. And so was the response he enjoyed: he hadn't really argued when his wife had suggested that power was the ultimate aphrodisiac.

Most of his staff were happy to seize the precious relaxation time afforded by the lunch hour to get away from their classrooms. The wide corridors of the modern school building were filled for a few minutes with the noise of newly released children. Then their teachers proceeded more soberly after them to their own recreation.

When Peter Logan stole softly into one of the science labs, it was deserted and silent. But the storeroom behind it was not. This little cell was small, almost claustrophobic, with a single high, square window, which let in a little light and revealed a tiny patch of grey, autumnal sky. But this was a private place, and privacy was what these two needed now.

She had taken off the white lab coat, as if discarding her working role for the lunch hour. Her face was glowing with a smile as he came into the little room. It lightened his heart to see it, and all the petty cares of the school day vanished in an instant. He was a young man again, almost as young as she was, when he saw that smile.

'I knew you'd come,' was all she said. Then they were in each other's arms.

Four

Peter Logan didn't really know everything that went on in Greenwood Comprehensive. It was a convenient fiction to put about, one which helped a headmaster to direct his staff and control his pupils more effectively. Logan knew that. And some of the people around him realized that the Headmaster could not possibly know everything. Some people, in fact, could even demonstrate that, if they chose to.

At the beginning of the new academic year in September, the school had a sixth form of over two hundred for the first time. That fact and its implications had been well documented in the local press. It meant more people preparing to go into higher education after school, more people striving to realize their full educational potential.

It also meant that there were more young people available as a market for those who were not interested in education at all.

Mark Lindsay was slightly surprised to be in the sixth form at all. His GCSE results were, he grudgingly admitted, a tribute to the teaching methods in the school. He didn't concede that at home, of course. He claimed there that his passes were entirely due to his own unremitting endeavour, and a fond mother – his father had departed with a younger model to North Yorkshire some years previously – believed him and looked forward to further triumphs of character.

Mark had not been expecting to make the sixth form. He had hesitated over whether he should take up the opportunity when it came. There wasn't much money at home, with his mother still working in the supermarket and his younger sister

21

at Greenwood Comp. Still only twelve. But no congenial employment had been on offer and his mother had been anxious for him to go on for A levels. In the end he had drifted into the sixth form.

But there were disadvantages to this new intellectual status. He had expected to have an income by now, to be swaggering home with a pay packet on Fridays. A lad of his age needed money. Other people knew that even more clearly than Mark did, and were prepared to do something about the situation.

To be precise, they were ready to exploit it.

Mark had taken to visiting Shakers club near the centre of Cheltenham on Friday nights. There were plenty of people he knew there: a few of his fellow sixth-formers among them, but also girls who had left the school in the summer and were now working in local factories or offices. They were now in that wide world outside school which people like Mark affected to know but in fact knew not at all. Most of the girls smoked a little, observing the dancing through small grey clouds of sophistication, affecting a slightly scornful sympathy for those still imprisoned within the world of school.

The teachers at Greenwood always referred to Mark Lindsay and his contemporaries as 'students' rather than pupils. It was a slightly clumsy and self-conscious acknowledgement of their new sixth-form status. On the other hand, the young women at the club, so much more important to Mark because of their erotic potential, still talked of 'school kids'. Moreover, they cast envious glances towards young men who were not only a year or two older than he was but had money in their pockets.

He watched these nineteen-year-olds, chatting to each other in words he could never catch above the music, nonchalantly ordering rounds of drinks he could not contemplate. These men seemed to Mark vastly sophisticated and worldly wise. He envied them, but did not see how he could ever emulate them. Money would be a start, but he could not see how

Saturday morning shelf-stacking in the supermarket was ever going to put him in their league.

He sat for a few minutes in a cubicle in the gents, glumly contemplating the paucity of what the lads would call his 'love life' when they compared notes on Monday morning. It was when he emerged from his little cell of contemplation that the first glimmerings of a solution presented themselves.

There was only one person in the small room: most of the Shakers' clients favoured the more modern and spacious toilets near the bars at the other end of the building. Mark went and washed his hands; he hadn't done anything in the cubicle except sit contemplating his lot in life with his hands in his lap, but he didn't want to start explaining that.

He hadn't looked at the other man in the tiled room: somehow you never did that when you were in the toilets. The man came and stood beside him now. Mark realized after a moment that this man wasn't washing his hands. Mark didn't turn to look at him but he glanced up into the big mirror above the washbasins to see if this silent companion was combing his hair.

He wasn't. He was completely motionless, studying Mark's actions; when his eyes met Mark's in the mirror, the lips below them relaxed slowly into a smile. There didn't seem to be much mirth in it, but Mark himself couldn't see anything to laugh at. He suddenly had an earnest wish that someone else would come into the room.

He forced an answering smile at the man and said, 'Quiet in here, isn't it?'

The man nodded. Mark wondered if this fellow had done something to ensure that they would not be disturbed. He'd seen people in films put 'Out of order' notices on doors when they went into toilets. Perhaps this man had—

'Quiet's the way we want it, for what we have to discuss.' The man's voice was low but clear, with an accent that did not belong to these parts: London, perhaps? It added harshly, 'It won't take long,' and the lips around it curled in a smile that was now openly contemptuous.

Mark wanted to say something insulting, to dismiss the man and flounce out of the room. Could men flounce? He didn't think they could. In any case, his tongue seemed suddenly frozen and he didn't think his legs could even attempt a flounce. He did the best he could by turning away from the washbasins and the face of the man in the mirror and went over to the roller towel on the wall. He was aware of the man at his side, but he put off looking at him for a long time, rubbing his fingers against the cotton of the towel until he thought it must disintegrate.

Eventually, he had to stop and turn sideways, as the man had known he must. He was lighting a spliff as Mark focused upon him again. The sweet smell of the cannabis seemed suddenly to fill the room. The man held it out for Mark, and Mark took it, put it between his lips, as if compelled by some hidden force. He wondered how the man knew that he had smoked cannabis.

Mark took a long pull at the spliff, letting the smoke fill his head, his lungs, his whole being. All resistance to the man and whatever he wanted seemed to disappear; he felt as he inhaled that he no longer wanted to hold out. But the stuff couldn't act as quickly as that, could it? Perhaps he just wanted to give up a struggle he knew he could not win.

The man's voice seemed to come not from beside him but from several yards away as he said, 'It's good stuff, isn't it?' He waited for Mark's nod of affirmation, for another pull on the spliff, before he said, 'There's plenty more where that came from.'

Mark nodded. It seemed the most natural thing in the world that there should be more of this on offer. He felt his mind relaxing in that knowledge. A small part of his brain still wondered what this man wanted with him, but it seemed easier not to fight him, not to summon up resistance which would have no effect. He said slowly, 'I expect there is. Plenty more.' Then he grinned, for his remark seemed to him highly sophisticated.

Mortal Taste

The man smiled again at him, more indulgently now. He had dark hair, cut very short, and a small gold earring. He took another spliff from his pocket and stuck it in the breast pocket of Mark's shirt, tucking it carefully out of sight, patting the pocket a little when he had finished. Then he said, 'You could have all the pot you wanted, you know, free of charge.'

Mark smiled. 'And what would I have to do for that?' He felt quite clever, negotiating with this man of the world, showing him that he knew nothing came for nothing.

The man smiled, seeming to acknowledge Mark as an equal, recognizing that he was dealing with a shrewd customer here. 'Offer us a little help, that's all. Become part of our distribution service.' He rolled off the phrase as if it amused him.

Mark wondered who the 'us' were. He didn't ask: something warned him that it was better not to know. He smiled again, to show he was no fool, that he would back out of this if he wanted to. He leaned a little towards the man. 'And who else is in your "distribution service"?'

A frown flashed quickly across the sallow features. Then the smile returned as the man said, 'That's for us to know and you not to know. You'll find it's better that way.' He nodded a couple of times and waited for Mark's answering nod before he said, 'There's money in it. Easy money. You could do with money, couldn't you, Mr Lindsay?'

Mark took another draw at the spliff, wondering exactly how much this man knew about him and his circumstances. He forced a little smile as he said, 'We can all use a little more money, can't we?'

The man nodded thoughtfully, as if assimilating a wise observation. Then he said, 'You wouldn't have to do much. There isn't an easier way of making money, for a lad like you.'

'How much money?'

The narrow shoulders shrugged, agitating the gold earring for a moment. 'Thirty quid, for starters. More, when you've

25

got the hang of things and begun to shift more. You'd be on commission, then.'

Commission sounded exciting to Mark, a glimpse of that bigger world outside which seemed so attractive to the girls he craved to touch. 'And I'd have stuff for my own use?'

'That's right. An allowance. Be up to you whether you smoked it all yourself or sold it on.'

'Just pot, is it?'

'Yes, just pot. Initially, at any rate. Smoking it is pretty well legal now, but we like to treat our distributors well.'

Mark finished the spliff. His head was singing and he knew he was high. But his brain seemed to be operating very sharply. He smiled at himself when he caught his image in the mirror. He felt as if he could handle this man and this situation easily enough, now. If you had the right sort of brain, pot just made you see things more clearly. He said, 'How would I get my supplies?'

The thin lips smiled. The man had the air of someone who had netted a small fish and was bringing it ashore, but Mark Lindsay was not able to see that. 'Don't you worry about that. They'll be there for you just as you need them. If you sell more, there'll be no difficulty about increasing the supply.'

'I see. Well, that seems satisfactory enough.' Mark could hardly believe this was him talking. He nodded a couple of times, imitating the businessmen he had seen on television, finding the gestures coming surprisingly easily to him. 'And who exactly will my customers be?'

'That's up to you. The lads and lasses in the sixth form, I should think, for a start.'

Mark liked the 'for a start'. And he thought he rather liked the 'lads and lasses' as well. That seemed to put him on a plane above them, looking down on them, using them as the unwitting pawns in his new business enterprise. With all the gravitas he could muster, he said, 'We'll need to be careful, you know.'

'Very careful. The pigs don't worry much about smoking

pot, but supplying it's still illegal, you know. And if you're successful, I expect you'll be going on to other things. E and coke, perhaps, if you get the customers. There's bigger money in that. But first things first.'

'First things first. That's right.' Mark repeated the words slowly, as if the sentiment was an important discovery for him. His fume-misted brain felt it could handle anything, now. He was dominating a boardroom, not standing in the toilets of Shakers.

The man controlled his impatience and his contempt, forcing another of his thin smiles, raising his hand for a moment to his earring, as if it helped him in complex thought. 'You can begin to test the ground. Carefully. If you're not sure of someone, you don't speak. Find a couple of punters who you're sure will want the stuff and sell to them. Other people will find out and come to you. That's the way it works. That way you don't take risks.'

'Don't take risks. That's right. That's the way we'll go about it.' Mark looked at himself earnestly in the mirror and nodded a few times, as if to tap home that message.

The man looked at him for a long few seconds, wondering if there was danger in this young fool. But he knew nothing. If he was caught, he couldn't tell the police a thing. He took the new recruit by the arm. Mark felt steely fingers pressing into his biceps, bruising him. He tried to twist away.

The man held on, increasing the pressure until the boy groaned. 'This isn't a paper round, son. There's easy money, but it doesn't come for nothing. You go carefully. And if you're stupid enough to get yourself caught, you say nothing. Absolutely schtum. Understood?' He brought up his second arm to emphasize his point to the pot-hazed brain, increasing the pressure on the boy's arm still further, his two hands like a band of iron on the puny bicep.

'Understood.' Mark Lindsay couldn't quite keep his voice steady on the word.

Five

On the Monday morning after his meeting at Shakers, Mark Lindsay looked speculatively round his fellow sixth formers, wondering which of them might become his first customers. He had come up with numerous possibilities over a frenetic weekend of consideration, but it was all more frightening, now that the time for actual decisions was approaching.

He was quite clear about one thing. He must be very careful to keep well clear of Peter Logan. That bugger seemed to know everything that went on around his school. There'd been a couple of sixth-formers last year who'd been found doing cannabis, and the Head had given them very short shrift indeed. If you were planning an enterprise like the one Mark had been offered, you'd need to be very careful indeed.

He would have breathed a little more easily had he realized that his head teacher was not even on the premises that day. Peter Logan was addressing a conference on Secondary School Organization in Birmingham. It was one of the penalties of success that you would be called upon for such things, as he had explained to his wife at some length on the previous evening.

The conference was on the Birmingham University campus. The weather was crisp and clear. Peter Logan enjoyed his walk from the car park to the Faculty of Education with a still blue sky above him. He was not worried about the talk he had to give, despite the fact that his audience would be composed of fellow head teachers, prospective head teachers and university professors of education. He had given the talk before; all he had done for this occasion was bring it up to date with the latest figures from his own school and a couple of references to the new guidelines from the Department of Education and Science.

Sure enough, when the moment came, his talk went well. He had set up the purpose-built Greenwood Comprehensive School from scratch and his address was basically an account of its development. He identified the initial problems he had faced and gave the details of how they had been solved. Then he went on to the development of the school over the last eight years. He catalogued the problems of growth. But growth, as he modestly pointed out, brought new resources, and his was basically a tale of success.

You didn't mention the ideas which you had tried and discarded when you found they did not work. You talked about the ones which had worked, and lit up the account with your own enthusiasm. That came easily enough, for Peter was genuinely excited by the task he had been set, the way he had gone about it, and the way in which he was continuing to work at it. Success in education was never absolute: you were always striving towards perfection, but never achieving it.

He livened up his story with a few shafts of humour, was even confident enough this time to detail one or two minor failures along the way. He kept his anecdotes real enough and near enough to the classroom for his address to seem practical advice rather than a retreat into the latest educational theories. He was glad to see that his fellow professionals in the schools as well as the ivory-tower academics from universities received him well.

There was animated conversation over a surprisingly good lunch at the end of the morning. Peter noticed that some quite senior figures in the educational world were seeking his company these days. He was human enough to be flattered by their attention.

It was the end of the lunch break before he could get away

to make a phone call. He found a small garden where he could use his mobile phone. 'It went well, I think.' He beamed modestly at the phone. 'The conference won't be finished until about six, I expect: there are discussion groups and then a reporting session. And there won't be much point in leaving before seven – I'll let the Birmingham rush hour clear itself. We country bumpkins aren't used to cut-throat driving! So I should be with you somewhere between eight and half past eight . . . No, the exhausted educationist will need reviving! . . . Well, I'll certainly look forward to that!'

Peter Logan gazed at his mobile phone fondly for a moment before he put it away. He looked up at the still clear blue sky above the city and saw that there was no one near him in this little patch of garden.

He wondered whether to ring his wife, but decided against it.

Jane Logan did not expect a phone call from her husband. She knew the pattern of occasions like this well enough: she was indeed, more aware of the sequence of days spent away from the school than Peter himself, who liked to think that he did not behave so predictably.

She knew that he was unlikely to return before ten thirty that evening.

Jane made an excellent evening meal for her daughter and herself, as though even food could be a defiant gesture against her husband's absence. She served it formally, wondering if her daughter would notice how much loving care had gone into the fresh trout, new potatoes and asparagus. Catriona tucked in with a healthy sixteen-year-old appetite and chatted cheerfully, seeming not to notice the food which disappeared so rapidly.

Catriona was at Greenwood Comprehensive, but she and her father avoided each other resolutely and successfully at school. The father wasn't going to court any accusations of favouritism, whilst the daughter was even more anxious to avoid any association with the man at the top of the pile. For the most part, she succeeded surprisingly well; her friends sometimes went several sentences through their ritual grumbling about the deficiencies in the school hierarchy before they remembered that Catriona had a connection.

It was easier for her because her elder brother had led the way, avoiding any accusations of sucking up to authority so successfully that he had been regularly disciplined for small misdemeanours throughout his school career. Matt was away at university now, his sister said grandly, as though to claim a little extra maturity herself from his progress. He was in fact attending the Freshers' Conference at St Andrews University at this very moment.

Catriona was a bright girl, who had performed impressively in her GCSEs this year and just entered the Greenwood sixth form. She was secretly determined to go to Cambridge, though she had not confessed quite how determined yet, even to her peers or her parents. She had a good relationship with her mother. They chatted easily about most topics, including things which went on at school.

It was through Catriona that Jane knew that quite a few of the sixth-formers were experimenting with drugs, and that soft drugs were now being used by people lower down the school, though not, she thought, in great numbers. Jane had told Peter about this and been met with a shrug of his broad shoulders. He was doing what he could to correct the situation. As usual, he gave nothing away about exactly how much he had discovered.

But all modern schools faced the problem: Greenwood was probably less affected than most of the larger comprehensives in the country. Peter Logan could not and would not use his daughter as a spy within the school, any more than he had used Matt before her.

Catriona knew the unwritten domestic codes as well as her father, and was happy with them. After five years in the school, she was well used to dealing with the problems arising from having her father as headmaster. In any case, she seemed to see less and less of him these days, and they rarely spoke of school affairs in their family conversations; both of them knew the ground which was dangerous and trod carefully around it.

It was easier with her mother. Neither of them were careful about boundaries, and they spoke happily and spontaneously . with each other. Catriona noticed that her mother rarely mentioned her father in their conversations these days. She wondered why that was.

'Dad's in Birmingham today, isn't he?' she said as she washed the dishes after their meal.

'Yes. I'm not expecting him back until quite late.' Jane dried the oval serving dish she had used for the trout and turned her back to put it away in the cupboard. She wondered whether to talk to Catriona about the vibrant new sixth form, with its record numbers and vast range of subject choices. Instead, she said, 'I think I'll go down to the gym again tonight.'

Her daughter grinned. 'You're becoming a real fitness freak, Mum! You'll be healthier than me, soon.'

Jane smiled fondly at her lithe daughter. 'No danger of that, kiddo! But we Yorkshire women like to get our money's worth when we join anything, you know.'

'I never used to think of you as a fitness fanatic.'

'Well, then, I can still surprise you, can't I? Anyway, I'm not a fanatic. It's just that you have to fight harder against the flab when you get to my advanced years. Have you never heard of middle-age spread?' Jane patted a stomach that was in fact reassuringly flat.

It was good to have a mother who did the things much younger women did, who could talk to you about teenage fashions, even if she was openly contemptuous of the sillier ones. Catriona called down a cheery goodbye from her bedroom as her mother left the house half an hour later.

It was curious that her friend's mother, who worked

part-time on the desk at the Gym Club, had never met her mother there.

Peter Logan drove fast down the M5. He was full of eager anticipation, and the motorway was quiet between seven and eight in the evening.

There was a crispness about the early evening darkness, and the lights going north on the opposite carriageway seemed unnaturally bright as they raced past him. He slowed for a few miles behind a police car, watching a small procession of cars build up behind him as others like him refused to exceed the speed limit to pass the official vehicle.

But the police Mondeo turned off at the Worcester exit and Peter eased his Rover 75 up to ninety, passing a succession of vehicles of various sizes, their red tail lights brilliantly sharp in the clear night air of early autumn. He wondered if there might be the first frost by morning; they were almost into October. It was pleasantly warm in the car and he was well aware of the danger of drowsiness after a full day. But he felt fully alert, not lethargic. It had been a successful day, and now there were the pleasures of the evening to look forward to.

He had met several of his contemporaries at the conference, people who had started to climb the educational ladder at more or less the same time as him. Not many had been as successful as he had. And some of them seemed to be slowing up a little. He had sensed an easing back on the throttle of ambition, a readiness to accept that not all goals were obtainable. Well, he still had his foot on the accelerator and a full relish for the ride ahead. He had discerned no diminution of his own energy, no slowing of his drive.

That went for all areas, leisure as well as work. He smiled in the darkness, fancied he felt a pleasurable stirring in his groin. You needed to play hard as well as work hard, if you were to be a proper man. The smile became a wide grin of anticipation.

It was pleasant travelling alone on an occasion like this. Even pleasanter when you controlled your own progress in a fast and comfortable car. He glanced at the car's clock as he left the motorway at Junction 16 and moved towards the suburbs of Cheltenham. He had made excellent time from the university campus in Birmingham. He slowed the big car to thirty miles an hour, which felt almost stationary after his motorway speeds. He would arrive before eight thirty, as he had promised; like many another man who lived much of his life by the clock, Peter Logan liked to be exactly punctual whenever it was possible.

He parked the car in the place he had chosen last time, two hundred yards from the flat he was visiting, by the side of a small park. It was not overlooked by houses, so there was little chance of any prying eyes noting its presence there. You couldn't afford gossip, in a job like his. People were still very old-fashioned in the moral view they took of headmasters and clergymen. It was unfair, but you might as well accept it.

He sat for a minute in the car when he had parked it, savouring the quietness of the spot he had chosen, feeling the excitement of the two hours which lay ahead. Then he eased himself from the driver's seat and pressed the automatic locking device on his key ring, watching the orange light flash brightly in the darkness as the doors were secured.

Peter Logan felt the pistol against his neck before he heard the terse phrases: 'Don't look round. Move forward, slowly.'

The voice was hoarse, perhaps with excitement. It was so near to his ear that it was distorted. Peter couldn't be sure whether it was male or female, but he moved obediently forward as the small, cold circle of steel pressed harder into his flesh. He couldn't believe this was happening to him. He suppressed an absurd urge to raise his hands above his head, as he had seen men do in Westerns. They moved a few yards, very slowly.

Peter Logan found his mouth very dry as he struggled into speech. 'Whoever you are, you've got the wrong man. I'm no threat to anyone. I'm the headmaster of a local school, that's all.' For once he didn't name it, didn't say that it was *the* local school. At this moment, he wanted his job to be as small and insignificant as possible.

The voice said, 'I know who you are, Logan. Move slowly and keep your arms by your side.'

Peter did as he was told. Perhaps this was some student prank to hold him to ransom for charity. Perhaps it was even one of his own sixth-formers on the end of a toy gun. He mustn't lose face.

The pistol felt horribly real.

The voice said, 'Turn right here. Keep your arms by your side. No abrupt movements.'

They were by a small gate which led into the park. With his head held rigidly and his eyes staring fiercely ahead, he had not seen it. He turned obediently into the blackness under the trees, wanting to stretch his hands out ahead of him, not daring to do so, in case any movement should be interpreted as aggressive.

Peter Logan discarded the idea that this was some student hoax. As he moved into the stygian darkness of the deserted park, fear flooded through him, retarding the movement of his limbs, paralysing his power of thought. He managed to gasp out, 'Look, if it's money you want, my wallet's in the inside pocket of my jacket. You're welcome to it!'

There were no words of response from behind him. Instead, the pistol pressed hard into the back of his head, driving him ever further into the darkness. He felt turf beneath his feet as he stumbled off the path, then threw up his hands to maintain his balance.

It was his last movement. His life disappeared into a blinding curtain of white pain as the pistol blew half his head away. He never heard the muffled sound which died in the foliage of the deserted park.

Six

D etective Sergeant Bert Hook should have been enjoying himself. He had finished work at midday. He was on a golf course, a very good one, the Worcestershire Golf Club at Malvern. A pleasant southerly breeze kept the temperature in the mid-sixties and moved high white clouds across a clear blue sky. The sun was just disappearing over the dramatic ridge of the Malvern Hills above the course. He could almost fancy he heard the strains of Elgar on the gentle down-draught from the hillside.

And yet the normally cheerful Bert Hook was not happy. Those who play the infuriating game of golf will know that it can often have that effect. A badly topped drive can make a man unconscious of Paradise around him. But Bert was not playing badly; indeed, for a man who had regarded the game with nothing but contempt until two years ago, he was playing quite well.

But he was partnering his old friend and working colleague, Superintendent John Lambert. And contemplating a venture into homicide.

The two were part of the Ross-on-Wye team that was playing the Worcestershire Golf Club in a C team fixture. 'It will be good for your game,' Lambert had said. 'Another new experience in your golfing development.'

It was. And Hook wasn't enjoying it.

As a detective, Bert had the greatest admiration for John Lambert. He had worked with him for twelve years now, and his respect for the man had grown with each one. When

36

they were on a case together, Hook worked for long hours and never counted the time. The chief was idiosyncratic in his methods, regarded as a dinosaur by some of the sharp young CID men who directed investigations from an office desk, but Bert Hook and the rest of his team showed him unquestioning loyalty.

On the golf course, it was very different. It was not that John Lambert was incompetent. Far from it: he enjoyed the status of an eight handicap, a level which Bert Hook aspired to but doubted if he would ever attain. The problem was that Lambert insisted on offering 'helpful' advice to his sergeant, whom he saw as a tyro in the game, a man who could and should benefit from his friend's experience.

After they had shaken hands with their opponents from the home club on the first tee, Lambert took Hook to one side. 'We're partners in the same team, so I'm allowed to offer you advice and guidance. And you mustn't hesitate to ask me for whatever help you need as we go along.'

Bert's heart sank to the soles of the new golf shoes he had bought for the occasion.

His fears were fully justified. Most of the trouble came on the holes where he was given a shot advantage. From his newly acquired nineteen handicap, Bert received eight of these. 'The difference in this match will come down to whether you use your shots or not,' Lambert explained with satisfaction on the second hole. He then stood at Hook's elbow with an almost maternal anxiety whenever Bert was playing one of his shot holes.

His tutoring became more elaborate and Bert's replies ever more terse as the match proceeded. Bert wished with increasing intensity that he had never given up cricket for this ridiculous pastime. The seam bowler who had terrorized the batsmen of Herefordshire and Gloucestershire for twenty years was being reduced to an incompetent by this effete game.

Well, not so much by the game as by his chief's advice on how to play it.

Matters came to a head with the match all square on the fourteenth. 'Swing easily, you're snatching at it,' Lambert advised the perspiring Hook. Bert tried. He made minimal contact with a ball which seemed to be growing smaller with each hole. It flew low and right and curled savagely into a ditch.

Lambert was there before his disgusted partner. He inspected the bottom of the ditch. 'There's hardly any water in there. You can get it out with a wedge, if you're careful. It's our only chance, now.'

Bert didn't like that 'now'. It was meant to remind him that all the partnership's troubles were down to this most recent disastrous shot. He stared unbelievingly at the top of his ball, just visible above an inch of green mire. He climbed obediently into the ditch, affecting not to notice the smirks of their opponents at this interesting development. To get anywhere near his ball, he had to bend like Quasimodo beneath a hawthorn. A vicious crop of steely thorns savaged his lower back and his buttocks. Nettles reared between his knees to threaten his manhood. He could no longer see his ball.

He reminded himself without conviction that he was doing this for pleasure.

Lambert's voice said from somewhere above him, 'You'll need to keep your head very still for this one. It's not an easy shot.'

By gingerly placing his left foot halfway up the bank of the ditch and leaning far to his right, Bert found that he could just see the top of his ball again through the undergrowth. He swung at it, hopelessly and without hope. His club caught in the branches of the hawthorn behind him, but with a desperate brute strength he wrested it clear and launched it at the ball. The steel of the club-head hit mud and stagnant water with an awful splatter and Hook's vision disappeared as a black wetness filled his eye-sockets.

He climbed heavily from the ditch, refusing to scream as the hawthorn scored his back and shoulders. There was spontaneous applause from his two opponents, with whom he had developed a rapport in the face of Lambert's assistance to him. He looked down and saw that the new trousers he had donned to represent the club in this, his first match, were spattered with evil-smelling black and green ditch water. There were ragged cheers and shouts of 'Encore!' from the four men in the match behind them.

Bert Hook limped towards his golf bag like a malodorous Dalmatian. He had slammed his wedge back into it before he realized the club-head was still covered with mud.

He was studiously avoiding any glance towards his partner. He took a deep breath and said, 'Where did the ball go?'

'It didn't come out of the ditch,' said Lambert sadly. 'I thought you were rather ambitious to attempt that shot, you know. When you've played a little longer, you'll realize what's possible and what isn't.'

It took two pints of bitter in the clubhouse to restore the usually equable Hook to anything approaching normal conversation with his chief. In the interim, he reflected sullenly that Lambert seemed worse since the news of his impending retirement had broken. He was bearing up bravely at work, even talking of time for hobbies, but Bert fancied sometimes that he detected a quiet sort of panic in the man he had worked with for so long.

Lambert would not have acknowledged anything so feeble in himself. But he was conscious of a restlessness, a refusal of his normally disciplined mind to settle to the tasks in hand. Perhaps it was because there was no really serious crime to occupy him at the moment. They had unearthed a tasty bit of embezzlement in a bank near the Welsh border, but that had now been passed to the Fraud Squad. He had only a little over two months of working life to go now and, in view of the irregular extensions Lambert had already been granted, even that was borrowed time. He was beginning to face up to the bleak prospect that his final murder investigation might be behind him.

Golf should have been a welcome relaxation. Yet whilst he kept his end up in the post-match conversation with their opponents, Lambert found it difficult to lose himself completely in the banter. When they trooped into the dining room for a very acceptable meal, he scarcely noticed what he was eating. Then he listened with only half an ear to the ritual speeches and rather desperate jokes from host team captain and visiting captain.

As soon as the formal proceedings were over, he wandered outside, away from the noisy hilarity which persisted in the clubhouse. The night was absolutely still, and surprisingly mild, considering that October was just around the corner. John Lambert moved away from the noise, a little way out on to the silent course, ignoring the dew upon his shoes. Here, all he could hear was the occasional hum of a car on the distant road along the base of the Malvern Hills, towering massively black above him.

There was a vivid sliver of crescent moon, quite low in the sky, and the stars sparkled as brightly as he had ever seen them. He felt very insignificant; his problems disappeared for a moment in the face of the futility of his very existence. There was not a movement in the huge oak trees to his left. The autumn colour was late this year, and there was no leaf fall beneath the canopies of branches. The trees were still 'those green-robed senators of mighty woods' which poor consumptive John Keats had registered almost two centuries ago.

John Lambert had lived twice as long as Keats already, and what had he to show for it? A few murderers put away, a few hundred villains locked up for a few years. It was an achievement of sorts, he supposed, but when the waters closed over him, his ripples would not last for very long.

'John?' Hook's voice from the doors of the clubhouse was barely audible.

Lambert turned hastily back towards the clubhouse. The interruption of his private reverie was unexpected but not unwelcome. He moved rapidly through the car park. 'I'm here, Bert. Enjoying a little solitude.'

'There was a call for you on the steward's phone. I explained that we couldn't use our mobiles in the clubhouse.'

Lambert's pulse quickened. This could only be serious crime, if someone from the CID section had sought them out here. 'What was it, Bert?' He was conscious of trying not to sound too eager.

'Some kids have found a body. Hidden under bushes in a park in Cheltenham. They think it's the headmaster of a big comprehensive school. He's been missing all day.'

'Suspicious?' But he already knew the answer to that.

Hook nodded, his face serious in the dim amber light from the open door of the clubhouse. 'Shot through the head, apparently. But not a suicide.'

Lambert didn't ask any more. There would be plenty of time for questions and speculation, in due course. In the meantime, he had his murder. Some poor fellow he had never known had been shot through the head. By person or persons as yet unknown.

Superintendent Lambert tried not to feel exultant as he went back to his car.

Seven

Christine Lambert found that her husband, who had been uncharacteristically lethargic of late, had finished his breakfast and was preparing to leave the bungalow when she came into the kitchen.

She glanced at the clock: it was still twenty minutes short of eight o'clock. She said, 'I thought you were winding down a little in your last few months. Getting ready for a life of leisure.'

'There's been a homicide in Cheltenham. At least, I'm assured it's a homicide.' He wondered if he sounded too satisfied with the news.

His wife nodded. 'The duty sergeant rang here last night. I told him you were playing golf at the Worcestershire.' Her voice was neutral now: years ago, she would have been full of resentment, hating the job whenever it interfered with his home life. Now, with the end of his career in sight, she was pleased to see him so animated again.

Twenty years ago, when they had had two young children and their marriage had been sailing perilously close to the rocks, John had made the situation worse. He had hugged the job to himself, offering few explanations for his lengthy absences from home, anxious to make his mark and build a career in CID work. Nowadays, in a profession notorious for its high divorce rates, the Lamberts' marriage seemed rock-steady and enduring to the youngsters in the service. Only under pressure, when he saw a young colleague with domestic troubles, would John Lambert reveal how near the partnership had been to coming apart.

He said, 'I didn't waken you when I came in last night. The post-match celebrations went on for rather a long time, I'm afraid.'

'Did you win, you and Bert?'

It was evidence of the way his mind had switched to his new preoccupation that he had to think hard about it. Yesterday seemed part of a different world. 'We lost, I'm afraid. I think I may have been a bit hard on poor old Bert. He didn't play very well.'

'I should think he's best left to his own devices, Bert. He's the kind of man who has to work things out for himself.' For a woman who had never played the game, who had never seen the two men together on a golf course, she was amazingly accurate. But she had been a gifted and perceptive teacher for thirty years. More important, she had known John Lambert for just as long.

'You may well be right.'

Lambert wondered whether he was concealing his impatience to be away. He was not.

Christine smiled as she turned away and fiddled with the toaster. 'You'd better get going. Murders not solved in the first week usually remain unsolved. I remember some things you tell me, you see.'

He said, 'I'll ring you if I'm going to be late,' and went gratefully out to his old Vauxhall Senator in the garage. They had never been a couple who kissed each other goodbye in the mornings.

Christine watched him turn the car in front of the bungalow and then drive briskly away. She made sure he was safely out of sight before she shook her head resignedly over the temperament of her husband.

There wasn't as yet much news on the death when Lambert arrived in the CID section at Oldford police station. The identity of the victim had been confirmed on the previous evening. A female officer had taken the widow to identify the body at the morgue in Cheltenham. Jane Logan had been shown the half of the face that was relatively undamaged, with the rest of what remained of the head carefully shrouded in layers of cotton sheet. She had signed the papers to confirm that this was what remained of Peter Logan, then collapsed in something very near to hysterics.

That was entirely understandable. Mrs Logan was now at home with her daughter. The doctor had given them both a sedative. The pathologist would be conducting the official post-mortem in the presence of a police officer first thing this morning.

The Chief Constable, Douglas Gibson, came in half an hour after John Lambert and called him up to his office. He wanted to talk about the new case but he began on a more personal note. 'I applied for an extension to your service, as you know, John.'

Lambert knew what was coming with that use of his forename. He had always got on well with the CC, who had indulged his Chief Superintendent's old-fashioned approach, recognizing him as a man who got results and put villains away. But Gibson was a formal man, as far as exchanges with his staff went. He was trying to sugar the pill with that 'John'. He went on quickly, 'It seems it's no dice, I'm afraid. I've heard nothing in writing as yet, but the bureaucratic grapevine tells me that my request will be refused.'

'Thank you for keeping me in touch, sir. I didn't expect anything else. If they made one exception, they'd have pressure to make hundreds.' Lambert noticed that he had retreated into using that convenient and anonymous 'they'.

'I expect they would. But I still think they should exercise a little discrimination about particular officers. I made out a very good case on the basis of the last ten years.'

'Thank you, sir.'

'It wasn't difficult. I'll reiterate my feelings, but I'm afraid it looks as though you must prepare yourself for retirement.'

Lambert smiled. 'I've been doing that, sir.' He didn't go in for rank much; he even forbade his own team to call him 'sir', except in formal settings. But somehow it seemed right on this occasion, as a means of putting an embarrassed CC at his ease. 'The roses are looking pretty good.' That traditional symbol of a copper's contented retirement. He sought desperately for something a little more original, and failed. 'I suppose I'll have no excuse for not playing better golf, when I'm able to play whenever I want to.'

Gibson shot him a wry, understanding smile. 'I hear you're pretty useful at the game already. Meantime, you've got a violent death to deal with.'

It was a signal that the CC was done with the awkward apologies about retirement. John Lambert as well as Douglas Gibson felt more at ease with an immediate problem. 'Yes, sir. I'm going out to look at the scene of the crime now. We should have the essentials of the PM findings by the end of the morning and the full written report by the end of the day.'

Gibson nodded. He had stood up and walked over to the window of his room whilst Lambert was speaking. He was looking out at the Gloucestershire landscape as he said, 'It's high-profile, John. "Sensational Death of a Highly Successful and Much-Loved Headmaster". You can hear the capitals as I say it. The nationals have already been on to me. I've given them a steady "No comment" so far, partly because I've bugger-all to tell them anyway. But I've had to agree to a media briefing at four o'clock this afternoon.'

'Do you want me there?'

Gibson was tempted. The self-effacing Lambert had acquired a reputation over the years, and showing him to the newshounds might mitigate the fact that he had little else that was useful to offer them. But he knew that Lambert hated sitting in front of cameras and journalists, and was well aware that he would be more usefully employed at the heart of the investigation than in a public relations exercise. 'No. I'll tell them our local super-sleuth is on the job! That may keep them at bay until we have something more tangible to offer them.'

Gibson stayed looking out of the window after Lambert had gone. He watched his Chief Superintendent and the more rotund DS Hook come out and drive away in the police Mondeo, eager as young CID novices to rejoin the hunt. He allowed himself an affectionate smile as he went back to his desk.

The Chief Constable would miss his Chief Superintendent when he lost him. Not for personal reasons, though he had grown to like as well as to admire the man. It was Lambert's expertise he would miss most. Douglas Gibson was a thief-taker still at heart, despite many years away from active police work. The Chief Constable wanted villains behind bars, and John Lambert had done more to put them there, more to improve the number of arrests for serious crime, than anyone else on this particular patch of England.

Gibson drafted a final letter pleading that Lambert should be made an exception to the retirement regulations. It wouldn't work; those faceless bureaucrats in London would have their way, but he would have done his best.

Meantime, he hoped fervently that John Lambert would win through on this last case.

There were a few curious onlookers around the point in the park where Peter Logan's body had been found, but not many.

This was partly because the uniformed constable guarding the scene from prying eyes was moving them on conscientiously, but rather more because there was nothing of interest to be seen. The copse of trees was cordoned off as an area of criminal investigation by the usual lengths of blue and white plastic tape, but what little activity there was within the rectangle was masked by the rather stunted trees.

Sergeant Jack Johnson, the SOC officer, was pleased to see Lambert picking his way into the cordoned area with the obligatory plastic bags over his shoes. Once the Superintendent had been and gone, he could pack up his equipment and take away his team and the scanty evidence they had gathered at the scene.

'There isn't much here, John. We've bagged everything we've found, but most of it is probably just the detritus of a modern public park and nothing to do with this killing. The photographer's already finished and gone.'

Lambert nodded, glancing automatically at the plastic bags at the edge of the area cordoned off. He saw a couple of beer cans, several ancient ice-cream or iced-lolly sticks, an array of carefully collected fibres which would probably prove irrelevant. A PC was putting a used condom into a bag at this moment. As he held it at arm's length with his tweezers, his young features filled with an almost comic distaste. 'Don't be so bloody squeamish, lad,' said Johnson in his old soldier's voice. 'You're lucky, handling it like that. Some poor sod at forensic's going to have to investigate the contents before he can chuck it away.'

'Did he die here?' said Lambert. The first and most important of the preliminary questions. If the corpse had been brought here and dumped after death, there would be a vehicle to search out, a possibility of bloodstains and other evidence from within it that might nail down a conviction quickly.

'He was almost certainly killed here, the pathologist thought. He had a good look before he allowed the corpse to be put in the meat wagon. Blood and other bodily matter found at the base of that tree apparently confirm that the shooting was here.'

Lambert and Hook looked automatically at the base of the stunted birch. 'Other bodily matter'. Brains, sinew, shattered bone. What had once made the thing which had been taken from here a man.

Johnson said, 'He might just have been moved a little, so that the bushes covered him more effectively. He'd been dead

47

for around twenty-four hours when he was found last night, the pathologist reckoned. But I've spent a good hour with the team around the entrance to the park where you came in. There's no sign that anything was dragged or carried through there.'

Lambert nodded. If Jack Johnson said nothing had come that way, then nothing had. He transferred his attention automatically back to the small, intimate cave of vegetation where they stood, trying to envisage exactly what had happened here. There was a moment of heavy silence before Hook said, 'It looks as if he arranged to meet someone here.'

But what would a successful, highly respected headmaster be doing meeting someone with a gun in a place like this? It was Johnson who voiced an even more chilling alternative. 'He might have been coerced to come here, of course. Someone might have decided in advance that this was a good place for a killing, might have brought him here in his car at gunpoint, or even forced him to drive himself here. His car was parked by the entrance. Forensic have taken it away to examine it.'

Lambert said, 'We'll need to find out if he'd any reason to be in the area of his own accord.' As usual, he was thinking practically, wondering where the resources of a large murder team might best be deployed. They would need house to house enquiries throughout the quiet roads around the park. Someone might have seen something in the darkness of that early autumn night; someone might be able to suggest a reason why Logan would have come here willingly.

Johnson interrupted his thoughts. 'He was shot at point-blank range. Through the back of his head.'

'What with?'

'No details of the weapon yet. Forensic might come up with something after the PM, I suppose, but there wasn't much of the head left to study. They did suggest that the entry wound indicated that there'd probably been a silencer on the murder weapon.'

'You haven't found the bullet?'

The SOC sergeant shook his head sadly. 'No sign of it in the SOC area. The top back of the head had gone completely. I'd guess a pistol was placed against the back of his head and fired with a slight elevation. The bullet may have continued onwards and upwards. Anyway, I'm satisfied it isn't anywhere in the immediate vicinity. We've looked hard enough.'

Hook looked at the ground in front of them, at the flattening of the sparse grass which indicated where the body had been found, at the sinister staining around the bole of the tree. 'How tall was he?'

He didn't need to explain the basis of his question to the old hands around him. Jack Johnson shook his head and said with a mirthless smile, 'He was over six feet, Bert. His assailant may have been only a little shorter. I'm afraid you can't assume it was a woman, or a resentful kid from his school.'

Lambert looked up at the quiet semi-detached houses by the park as they left. He had a curious sensation that he had sometimes experienced before that their killer was watching their efforts, was smiling mockingly at their minimal progress. But the houses might have been unoccupied; their fronts looked square and unhelpful, their windows were as blank and unfocussed as blind eyes. There was no twitching of a curtain to indicate a curious watcher, no sign of the nosey parker who might have witnessed useful things thirty-six hours earlier.

Lambert had the feeling already that this was going to be a complex case.

Eight

There was a curious air of subdued excitement hanging over Greenwood Comprehensive School.

Lambert and Hook felt it as soon as they got out of the police Mondeo in the staff car park. The weather was warm for the last day of September, but there had been no sun for several hours and the atmosphere was heavy under low cloud. There was not much movement evident in the place during the last hour of the school day, but a febrile, almost guilty, expectation hung over everyone who greeted them. The staff and the students of Greenwood were still absorbing the unthinkable tidings of their leader's death. Now they were waiting to see how the police would go about exposing his killers.

A tall woman with blonde hair met them before they could reach the Secretary's office. 'Pat Dean, Deputy Head,' she said tersely. 'Thank you for your phone call. Needless to say, we're all still very shocked. Needless to say also, we want you to find out who killed Peter, as quickly as possible.' She said this while taking them into the privacy of her office, as though even that short journey must be filled with assurances of support.

When they were sitting on the armchairs in her room, she said guiltily, 'I can organize some tea. It's just that – well, as you can imagine, it's been a rather disjointed few hours.' The acknowledgement of that seemed almost a relief to her, and they divined that she had lurched from crisis to crisis in the organization of this fraught school day.

Lambert was as anxious as she was to get things under way. 'No tea, thanks. We'll need to speak to all your staff, as quickly as we can. It will probably be necessary to have at least a collective word with your sixth-formers. Depending on the progress and the direction of the investigation, we may have to come back into the school, to follow up statements from different individuals.'

'I understand that. All I ask is that you keep things as low-key as possible. I've had the press vultures on the phone all day, whilst I've been busy with other things. I fear they'll be waiting for the children outside the gates when they leave the school this evening.'

'We've already arranged for male and female PCs to patrol the school exit for the hour from four to five. I can't guarantee that the more unscrupulous newshounds won't follow children home, trying to get quotes from them or their parents. This will be big national news, for at least a couple of days.' His long face cracked into a grimace of distaste for the transience of journalistic tragedy, and the tall woman behind the big desk warmed a little to him for it. He said, 'I believe Mr Logan's own children attend the school.'

'The elder one, Matthew, has just finished here and gone off to university. Catriona, the daughter, has just entered our sixth form. But as you'd expect, she isn't in today. I'm not expecting her to be around for the rest of the week. It will be better for the rest of us in the school as well as Catriona if we're allowed a period away from each other.'

'We need to get our questioning under way as soon as possible.'

She nodded. 'I've arranged for the staff to gather in the assembly hall at the end of afternoon school. It's more neutral ground than the staff room.'

'Thank you. And thank you for your time now. I appreciate how busy you must be. We'll be as unobtrusive as possible, but we're bound to disrupt the life of the school to some extent.'

Mrs Dean gave them a rueful smile. She was no more than forty-five, her strong face more attractive because of her air of concentration. 'That's already happened, as you can well imagine. But I'm grateful for your consideration. The sooner we can get the school back into a normal routine, the better it will be for everyone. If you can disturb that routine as little as possible, we'll all get on with life as well as is possible under the circumstances.'

Lambert nodded. 'We'll keep things as low-key as we can. In the meantime, you may be able to help us to get things under way on the right lines. You were Mr Logan's Deputy Head; you must have known him very well.'

'We had a very close professional relationship, yes.'

She put a stress on the word 'professional' and they knew immediately that she was putting a little distance between herself and the dead man. Lambert decided to press on and ignore that. 'So you must have had some immediate thoughts on who killed him. We'd like you to relay those reactions to us in the few minutes we have before we meet your staff.'

Pat Dean said stiffly, 'My first reaction was one of outrage that anyone should do such a thing to Peter. It remains so, even after hours of hectic activity in the school today. I have no notion who might have killed him. It seems strange to me that you should expect me to have any such idea.'

'Not so strange, surely.'

'In so far as I have thought about the details of Peter's death at all, I have assumed it was a random piece of violence. You would no doubt agree that there are plenty of those in the world today. Not least because the schools and the police, rather than the society which employs us, get blamed for most of them.'

Lambert gave her a small, companionable smile at the comment, wondering whether it was a stock reaction or a diversionary tactic. 'Very few pieces of serious violence are random, I'm afraid. There are three possible connections with this killing. Mr Logan's home life, his working life, or some secret private life outside both of those. The home life and the working life are much the most likely areas of connection. Hence our presence here this afternoon.'

She looked at them for a moment, then nodded reluctantly, as if accepting the logic of his assertion. 'I shall be extremely surprised if Peter Logan's death was connected with his life in the school.'

'So you can't immediately suggest any members of your staff to whom we should give particular attention?'

'No. My relationship with Peter was a close professional one. Like everyone else, I am full of admiration for what he has achieved at Greenwood. But we didn't see much of each other outside working hours. I've met his wife on school occasions but, as I say, Peter and I didn't socialize much outside our work. No doubt you will unearth people in due course who can tell you much more than me about the private side of Peter Logan's life.'

She had a few more ideas than she was admitting to, Lambert was sure, but this wasn't the moment to press her. The school bells were ringing for the end of the day. And he was going to need this woman's co-operation as his murder team came and went within the school during the next few days.

He contented himself with saying, 'Possible lines of inquiry may suggest themselves to you, when you have had a little more time to yourself. Please get in touch with me person-ally if they do, even if the people involved seem most unlikely possibilities.' Without meaning to, he had spoken as stiffly as she had.

Ten minutes later, she took them into the school's assembly hall to meet the staff. Lambert had asked that all the ancillary staff, the lab assistants, clerical staff, librarians and caretakers should come as well as the teaching staff. There were over a hundred people in the room. Schools had become a lot larger since his day, he thought ruefully.

It was rather like addressing a public meeting. Lambert

explained that members of the CID team would be collecting preliminary statements from most of the people in the room over the next twenty-four hours. He was certain that everyone was as anxious as he was that the perpetrator of this brutal killing should be brought to justice as swiftly as possible. To that end, anyone who had any thoughts on the murder, however outlandish they might seem, should stay behind now and talk to him immediately.

In particular, he would be interested if there was anyone in the room who could throw any light on why their late head teacher had gone to the park where he had been killed. There was an electric silence after this request. He caught one or two swiftly exchanged glances among his audience. He invited questions or observations, but received none.

No one came to speak to him when the meeting broke up.

'Go away! Just bugger off, will you! We've nothing to say, so leave us alone!' The youth had desperation in his voice. Having to act as the man of the house had come too suddenly for him.

'We're not press,' said Lambert sympathetically, showing his warrant card. 'I'm sorry we have to come at a time like this, but we do need a few words with your mother.'

The young man hesitated, looked for a moment as if he would bar their way. From the hall behind him, his mother's voice said, 'It's all right, Matt. Let them in, if they're police.'

The youth stood back and motioned them past him, looking anxiously down the drive for the journalistic jackals who were not there. Then he followed them into the hall and said, 'I'm sorry. They've been hanging around all day. I'm trying to keep them away from my mother and Catriona.' Bert Hook felt very sorry for him. He was trying hard to behave like a mature man, and paradoxically it made him look more of a boy. Having ushered them into the room, he stood self-consciously beside them with his weight all on one leg. Then he self-consciously folded his arms; he looked like an actor trying to play an older man in a school play.

The sitting room had a scattering of empty cups and mugs on most of its flat surfaces. Matt eventually went and took up his position by his mother, so that she was framed by daughter and son, standing stiffly on either side of her like protective sentries. Perhaps the older woman, even in the distress they were trying to defend from outsiders, recognized something ridiculous in this little tableau, or perhaps the little smile was the conditioned middle-class reaction, welcoming strangers, however intrusive, into her home.

She said, 'You will have gathered that I'm Jane Logan. This is my daughter, Catriona, and my son, Matt.' The boy moved half-forward to shake hands with the introduction, then realized that this was not an occasion for that. He stood uncomfortably gauche, with his left hand by his side and his right one still half-extended towards the CID men. He said, 'Can't this wait? Surely you don't need to push your way in here on this of all days.'

Lambert said, 'I'm afraid it can't. We can leave a more formal interview until later but we need to ask one or two preliminary questions immediately.'

Matt would have protested further, but his mother said calmly, 'You'd better sit down,' and set the example by doing so herself in the middle of the wide sofa. Her children hesitated, then sat down one on each side of her, while Lambert and Hook planted themselves gratefully in the two armchairs opposite them.

Jane Logan looked quite composed, with her fair hair perfectly in place, despite the strain around eyes which had probably been tearful for most of the day. The younger face of Catriona Logan at her side seemed more puffed with grief, more tremulous than hers, but this was probably the first real tragedy in a young girl's life. Lambert said, 'Just a few initial questions, as I said. I understand Mr Logan was in Birmingham on the day of his death.'

'At a one-day conference on trends in secondary education, yes,' said Jane Logan.

'He was giving one of the papers in the morning,' said Catriona, her pride in her dead father peeping through her ravaged face.

'Dad was something of an authority on comprehensive schools, you see,' said Matt, anxious to support his sister.

'So I understand. My wife's a teacher: she told me how eminent your Dad was.' Lambert smiled from one to the other, then said to the woman in between them, 'Was he staying overnight in Birmingham?'

There was a tiny pause before she said, 'No. But I wasn't expecting him back until late. Ten thirty or eleven, perhaps.'

'You didn't report him missing until the next morning, though.'

Perhaps it sounded like an accusation, for Catriona put her hand upon her mother's, would perhaps have spoken if Jane Logan had not said calmly, 'No. I just presumed Peter had been delayed by something. I went to bed at eleven and promptly fell asleep. It wasn't until the next morning that I realized that Peter hadn't come home.'

Catriona said protectively, 'Mum had been to the gym that night after a day's work. She was tired out,' and her mother smiled her affirmation, as if a little embarrassed by the unnecessary detail.

Lambert would have liked to ask her mother a supplementary question, but that would have to wait. Instead, he said, 'I'm sorry to have to bring you these details now, but it appears that your husband was killed by person or persons as yet unknown. You know where he died. Have you any idea why he should have been visiting that area of the town at that particular time?'

'No. None at all.'

Her denial came so promptly that her son glanced sharply

sideways at her. Matt said, 'Wasn't Dad taken there under duress by someone? That's what we assumed.'

Lambert said, 'He might have been. I'm afraid we know very little about the circumstances of the death yet. Your father might have been compelled to go there. He might have arranged to meet someone in that park, someone who then chose to kill him. He may even have gone there for some other purpose entirely, and been surprised by the person who killed him. We shall know more in a few days, but only by asking questions such as this. Eventually we shall find someone who can offer us significant information.'

The boy nodded, digesting it carefully. He said inconsequentially, 'I came home from the Freshers' Conference at university as soon as I heard. But we don't know why Dad was there, do we, Sis?' He spoke as though they might have known things their mother did not; it was probably just that he had been discussing why his father should have been in the park while he was alone with Catriona during the day. The girl shook her head to support him, while her mother remained still as a statue between them.

Lambert said, 'Just one more question, then we'll leave you in peace. A simple one, for all three of you, if you like. Can you think of anyone who might have wished to offer Mr Logan this sort of violence? Each of you knows far more about the life he led than we do, who never even knew him. It doesn't matter how unlikely any suggestion you make may seem. If it proves baseless, it will go no further than this room.'

The three faces opposite him looked from one to the other. Jane Logan was beginning to shake her head when her daughter said suddenly, 'There are drugs at the school, you know. I don't know where they come from, but someone's making a lot of money out of supplying them.'

'No more than any other school!' said her mother sharply, as if she needed to defend the reputation of a man who could no longer defend himself.

'They were there though, Mum,' said Matt quietly. 'Dad knew about it. He was trying to do whatever he could to control it.'

'It's a good thought,' said Lambert. 'Every secondary school has its problems. I would say Greenwood's are less severe than those of many schools of the same size, but there are inevitably some pretty nasty characters in the background. Well in the background, unfortunately, but we shall be looking for any connection.' He looked again at Catriona. 'You're the only one currently in the school. Can you give us any more definite information about the drugs being sold?'

'No. I've always kept well clear of them myself.'

Matt came in quickly. 'And being the headmaster's kids, the pushers have always kept well clear of us!'

Catriona said, 'I'll keep my ear to the ground when I get back to school next week. There must be people in the sixth form who know much more than me about it.'

Bert Hook glanced at Lambert and said, 'Please don't do that. There are dangerous people involved in the drugs trade. They won't come anywhere near the school, because it's small beer to them. But if they hear you're playing amateur detective, there could be more violence.'

Lambert nodded. 'You wouldn't get anywhere, in any case, Catriona. It's such a dangerous part of the criminal world that even the police have to have specialists. The Drugs Squad are quite separate from us. I shall be in touch with them over the next few days, to try to find out whether your father's death has a drugs connection. If you hear anything you think is useful, we'll pass it on, of course, but please heed what DS Hook says. Don't get involved with trying to find out where the drugs are coming from.'

Jane Logan put an arm round each of her children and drew them close, as she had been used to do when they were much younger. 'Listen to that, kids! One death in the family is quite enough. I don't want to lose anyone else.'

Lambert and Hook left them like that, seeing themselves swiftly out of the house. The memory of that touching family triptych, with the mother protective of her issue, stayed with Lambert far into the night.

It would not have been possible to question Jane Logan further in front of her children. That was a pity, because he would have liked to follow up the one lie he was certain she had already told them.

He watched his hands tremble as he put in the number. He had not realized he was as nervous as this: he had to make three attempts before he was satisfied that he had tapped out the right figures.

The number rang three, four, five times, seeming to his heightened senses to take a long time to do so. He had almost given up hope of a response when the phone was picked up.

He was too distraught to introduce himself. 'They've been into the school!' he said, his voice sounding strangely hoarse in his own ears.

'Who's "they"?'

'You know who I mean! The police. They've been into the school. After lessons were over, today.'

'So what? You knew they were coming. Standard practice. Start in the victim's home and workplace.'

'You know how they proceed with things like this?'

'Course I don't. I use my common sense, that's all. It's what I'd do, if I was a copper, which God forbid!'

The voice allowed itself a snigger at the ridiculous nature of that thought, and he felt himself panicking. 'You're not taking this seriously!'

'No!' The voice was suddenly harsh with authority. 'You're taking it *too* seriously, that's all. Just keep your head, or you'll have us all in trouble. Do you hear me?'

'Yes. Yes, you're right. They don't know anything about us, do they?'

'No they don't, and it's your job to keep it that way.'

'It's easy to say that. You're not in the firing line!'

'And I'd better not be, either!' There was a pause, perhaps to let the warning sink in. Then the voice came back in a less minatory tone. 'What did the police say?'

'It was two CID men, a superintendent and a sergeant, I think. They assembled all the staff in the main hall, ancillaries as well as teachers. They just asked if any of us knew anyone who might have wished to have Logan out of the way.'

'And did anyone come up with any suggestions?'

'No. Not while we were all together in the meeting, anyway.'

'Well, there you are then. You've nothing to fear.'

'But they invited anyone who had any thoughts to stay behind and talk to them privately. And they said that police from the murder team will be seeing each of us individually. Taking statements.'

'Standard practice, again. Don't you ever watch crime series on television?'

'No. Can't say I do.'

Another snigger. 'Too busy with your naughty videos, I expect. Good, that last one, wasn't it?'

'Yes. I – I wish I'd never bought it though, now.'

'Can't turn the clock back, can we? And it's foolish to try. Just keep your head down and say nothing and you'll be all right. "The only thing we have to fear is fear itself." Know who said that?'

'No, and I don't think at this moment that—'

'Franklin D. Roosevelt. Good old F.D.R. Bit of a lad himself, you know, old F.D.R. was. Got things done, though, didn't he?'

The last phrase rang ominously in his head. He decided to ignore it. 'What do I say when they question me?'

'Just play it straight. Tell them nothing. They've no reason to suspect you of murder, have they?'

'No, I suppose not. But where do I say I was on Monday night when he was being killed?'

'There you go already, saying more than you need to say. How do you know he was killed on Monday night?'

'The paper said so, I think.'

'You *think*? Hell, that's no good! Just don't give anything away. Let them make the statements, give you the information. You say yes, no, I don't know. Play schtum. Hell, it's easy enough, isn't it?'

'It sounds it, when you put it like that. But you're not going to be in the hot seat, are you?'

'And neither are you. You mustn't even think of it like that. You're just one of fifty-odd members of the teaching staff being routinely questioned. The more boring you can make it, the less you'll stand out and the quicker they'll give up.'

'All right. I'll do my best.'

'You'll do more than that. You'll make sure they think there's nothing worth following up.' The threat in the voice was unmistakable now as it tried to stiffen the resolve of the listener. 'There's more than you will suffer, you know, if they get interested in our activities. And some of us wouldn't be very pleased with you if you let us down.'

'All right.' He stopped himself just in time from saying again that he would do his best. He was suddenly anxious to terminate the conversation he had initiated himself. 'As you say, it shouldn't be too difficult, if I'm careful.'

'Don't get too clever. Don't try to send them down false trails. You'd like to be helpful, but you know nothing.'

The voice was itself suddenly worried, anxious to guide him along the paths which would keep all of them out of trouble. But it was too late for that. He had had all the advice he could take. He made a hurried thanks and rang off.

He looked stupidly at the phone for a full minute. He still hadn't solved the problem of what he was going to say if the police asked where he'd been on Monday night. Nevertheless, he should be safe enough, if he was careful, he told himself unconvincingly.

He would need to be at his most alert tomorrow. But he wondered whether he could risk two of his sleeping pills tonight.

Nine

There was a fulsome obituary of Peter Logan in *The Times* on Thursday morning. In the past, that august organ had noted the passing of head teachers only when they had reigned in the great private schools of the land. Now, rejoicing in his new egalitarian clothes, the *Times* writer eulogized the contribution Peter Logan had made to the enrichment of thousands of Gloucestershire lives.

. . . No one had heard of Cheltenham's Greenwood Comprehensive school when Peter Logan went there ten years ago. Operating almost in the shadow of two great and famous private educational institutions, Logan set about building up a school which would embody all that was best in modern education.

His guiding principle was the simple but noble one of enabling each child that came into his school to develop fully whatever potential lay within him or her. Sometimes that potential would be obvious, sometimes it would have to be discovered by sensitive teachers and carefully nurtured.

The result of this philosophy was that the achievements of many of Greenwood's pupils surprised their teachers, their fond parents, and not least themselves. When Logan took over, his school was in effect one of those secondary modern schools which have been given a slightly wider intake area and designated a comprehensive. It had some 400 pupils, none of whom stayed on beyond the age of sixteen. A small number transferred after GCSEs to a sixth-form college or into further education.

Logan lobbied for and secured his own sixth form. Last year well over a hundred of Greenwood's leavers went into higher education. The school's sixth form now has over 200 members pursuing a vast range of courses. It has risen from obscurity to become a national model for secondary school development. Unlike some educationists, Logan welcomed the advent of the controversial 'league tables' to measure the progress of schools, and saw his beloved Greenwood rise steadily towards the top layers of achievement . . .

There was much more in the same vein, but little which gave Lambert, reading the piece over his early breakfast, any clue to those darker elements of human existence which might have brought Logan close to the violence which had so abruptly terminated this life of achievement. Apart from the initial brief account of Logan's humble childhood and student career, the obituary was a record of public achievement rather than of private strengths and frailties. That was how these things should be, he supposed gloomily, but it wasn't a lot of help to policemen who had never known the man.

He took his mug of tea out into the garden, wandering round the roses and the last of the dahlias, scarcely seeing the blooms he had been watching so closely last week, before Logan's death had pitched him into the world of education, of which he felt he knew so little.

He said as much to Christine when he went back into the bungalow. 'You know more than most,' she grinned at him. 'You've heard me moaning enough about class sizes over the last few years.'

'That doesn't tell me what his staff thought about Peter Logan.'

She thought for a moment. 'No doubt they bitched about

him in private. The great man taking all the plaudits whilst they did all the work. The man at the top more concerned with public relations than with the problems of his staff. Talking expansively about the school to people outside whilst ignoring the fact that three of his staff were on maternity leave and the supply teachers weren't up to it. That sort of thing.'

It sounded so like the police world that he knew that it cheered him a little. People were much the same, wherever they worked, and he had got to know quite a lot about people in the last thirty years. Perhaps it was the seamier side of human nature that he had explored most thoroughly, but that was the side he would need now, if he was to answer the *Times* leader's plea for 'justice for this educational hero cut down in his prime.'

He was reassured to find that the machinery of the investigation was humming busily when he got into the CID section at Oldford. DI Chris Rushton was already feeding a steady stream of information into his computer. Six officers would be taking preliminary statements in the school throughout the day. Uniformed officers had already on the previous evening begun a house to house inquiry in the streets around the park where Logan had died. The full PM report would be delivered within the hour.

Although his natural inclination was to be out and about, Lambert was cheered a little just to be at the centre of things for a few minutes. Somewhere from this mass of information and ant-like activity something significant must surely emerge.

Dennis Ingram, the Conference Organizer at the University of Birmingham, led an exacting but rather dull life. The variations in his working day were not normally exciting ones. His work did not demand a vivid imagination. So when his personal assistant told him that there was a policeman wanting to speak to him urgently, he nodded resignedly, seeing this as just another chore to be added to an already crowded day.

When he found that he was a part, however peripheral, of a murder investigation, Dennis was secretly delighted. Even in an increasingly violent world, the word 'murder' still carries a unique, grisly glamour. To be questioned about the movements of a man who had given an address to the great and the good in education in the main conference room at the beginning of the week gave a frisson of excitement to a humdrum Thursday morning. Especially now that he knew that the man had never reached home on that Monday evening.

He was a little disappointed in the representative of the law sent to see him, a stolid man with a weather-beaten country face who introduced himself as Detective Sergeant Hook. Perhaps this was a man more used to putting nervous interviewees at their ease than generating excitement, Dennis thought, as Hook took him calmly through an account of the previous Monday's conference which made it seem very pedestrian.

It was the questioning at the end of this, where Hook concentrated upon the central figure in the investigation, which made Dennis think later that he might after all have contributed something to the case.

'So you were at the back of the hall throughout Mr Logan's morning address to the conference members?' said Hook when he had a picture of the day.

'I popped in and out at the back of the hall, actually. I wanted to check that the arrangements for lunch were running smoothly. But I was there for most of Mr Logan's address. "Trends in Secondary Education" was the title. I found it quite interesting, really, because he was a very good speaker.'

'And did he seem at all nervous? I'm thinking of before and after the lecture, rather than during the actual address.'

'No. I met him when he arrived and showed him to the rooms we were using, and I mingled with the conference members when they had a glass of wine before lunch. He seemed happy and outgoing on both occasions – certainly not nervous.' Ingram delivered his phrases with a prim precision, as if he was choosing his words carefully for a court of law; perhaps that is what he envisaged as the eventual outcome of this.

'And you say you didn't see him during the afternoon.'

'No. Most of that was spent in small groups, discussing issues raised earlier in the day. Then the conference members came back together for a plenary session at four fifteen, after a break for a cup of tea. I didn't see Mr Logan at all during the afternoon. But I saw him before it began.' Dennis produced the information with a modest flourish; he had been waiting for this moment.

Hook didn't mind people playing up the drama a little, so long as they told all they knew. He asked patiently, 'Before the afternoon sessions?'

'Yes. I was relaxing after lunch; to tell you the truth, I was rather relieved that everything seemed to be going so well. I went out into the gardens behind the dining room for a breath of fresh air. It was a bright day for late September, and I sat down for a couple of minutes on one of the benches. I remember thinking that we wouldn't get many more opportunities this year to sit in a warm sun.'

'And that is when you spoke to Mr Logan?'

'I didn't actually speak to him, no.' Ingram's disappointment was evident in his face. 'He was at the other side of the gardens and I don't think he even noticed me. But I did see what he was doing.'

'Which was?'

'He made a call on his mobile phone. We don't permit the use of them in the conference centre, but people often slip outside to use them.'

'Did you hear what he said?'

Ingram was torn between being aghast that someone would even consider that he might eavesdrop and mortification that he could not offer key evidence in a murder hunt.

Mortification won. He said, 'I'm afraid I didn't hear anything he said. As I said, he was at the other side of the gardens.'

'Did he make one call or several?'

'Just the one.'

Hook made a note of that in his clear, round hand. Probably just a routine call in a busy headmaster's day. But it would have been interesting to know to whom Logan had been speaking. The school hadn't had a call from him, and Jane Logan hadn't mentioned any calls from her husband during their brief meeting with her last night. 'And you didn't see him again during the day?'

'No. Well, not until the conference was over, anyway.'

Hook concealed his irritation. 'But you talked with him then?'

'No. It was in the evening. The rest of my staff had gone home, but we had another, smaller gathering in the Conference Centre the next day. I was just checking that everything was in place as it should be before I went home.'

Hook nodded. 'Anal' they called it nowadays; twenty years and more ago, when he had joined the police service, it would have been 'conscientious'. 'So what time would this be?'

'Ten to seven.' The reply came promptly: Ingram had suddenly realized that he might have been almost the last person to see Peter Logan alive. He could see himself making this statement in a crowded court.

'Did you speak to him?'

'No. I waved to him across the car park, that was all. He was getting into his car as I came out. I followed him out in my own car and drove behind him until our routes diverged.'

'Do you think he was going somewhere local?'

'No. He was within a mile of the M5 when I turned off. I expect he'd let the rush-hour traffic get away before he left. He'd have been back home in Cheltenham by eight to half past.'

Except he wasn't, thought Bert Hook. And his wife hadn't

68

been expecting him until ten thirty or eleven. Or so she said.

Superintendent Lambert wasn't in the station when the man asked to speak to him. But as soon as he claimed he knew something about the death of Peter Logan, he was ushered straight in to see Detective Inspector Rushton. Murder opens doors faster than a skeleton key.

He was about thirty, with hair which he seemed to have forgotten to comb and clothes which made him look as if he had been dressed by a mother with other things on her mind. He had a wild look in his eye, which made Chris Rushton fear the worst; this could be one of those weirdos whom every high-profile murder brings into police stations up and down the land. He was almost certainly on drugs; he would probably be confessing in the next five minutes.

Chris decided to interview him in the open CID section, with other officers coming and going around them. It would be easier to get rid of him from here than from an interview room when he proved a useless distraction from the business in hand. And there is always a possibility that nutters will turn violent when they sense you aren't taking them seriously.

Whilst Rushton's spirit sank within him, he was icily polite on the surface. 'I'm told you have information connected with the death of Peter Logan. We are grateful for anything the public can offer, at this early stage of the investigation. But you will appreciate how busy we are.' He gestured vaguely at the hum of activity around him, and received a gratifying nod of acceptance from the man in front of him. 'You'd better sit down for a moment.'

'It won't take long. I thought you ought to know.'

Chris pulled a pad out in front of him. He normally worked straight on to a computer now, but people like this were often quelled by a blank sheet of paper, by the sight of their wilder ramblings being recorded and preserved. 'Name?'

'Darcy. Darcy Simpson.' He watched Rushton hesitate

over the first name and said, 'I don't usually bother with any apostrophes. It's my mother's fault, you see. She was a Jane Austen fan.'

'Occupation?'

The mobile, too expressive features registered disappointment, then confusion. 'Nothing, at the moment, I suppose. I worked on a building site, last month.' Darcy Simpson looked at the inspector to see if he was impressed by that, as he obviously was himself. 'I trained as a teacher of art, taught in a school for a while. But that's years ago now.' He gazed unseeingly at the wall behind Rushton, as if he saw for a moment another man in another life.

Rushton took down a few more details. At least he had an address. Rushton told him not to leave it without letting them know where he was going. Might as well play it by the book. Chris was a great one for the police book: it had elevated him to an Inspector's rank when he was scarcely past thirty, though he suspected it had cost him his marriage at the same time.

The routine of detection said that at this stage of a case you had to consider the unlikely as carefully as the probable. It was still possible DI Rushton would prove to be the officer who had drawn out the key information in the case from this man, the officer who had spotted the possibilities in an unlikely source. He finished his writing at the bottom of the sheet and looked up again at the unpromising figure in front of him. Only just possible.

'So you think you can help us find who killed Mr Peter Logan. You knew him, did you?'

'No, I never met him.'

Rushton's faint hopes fell still further. 'Mr Simpson, we're really very busy with this investigation—'

'But I know someone on his staff. Someone who teaches there.'

'There are over fifty teachers at Greenwood Comprehensive School. Unless you've got good reason to think that—'

'Tamsin Phillips. Teaches history. I used to live with her.' Simpson was becoming more and more excited.

Rushton wondered how he was going to calm him, then get rid of him. Other officers were already watching them curiously. He wasn't good with nutters, never had been. Perhaps he should have chosen somewhere more private for this exchange, after all. He tried to find a soothing tone. 'That is very interesting, I'm sure, but I fail to see that it has any bearing on—'

'I think she killed him. Tamsin Phillips.' His eyes flashed wildly.

'Now that is a very serious accusation to make, Mr Simpson. Darcy. I think you should consider—'

'She's been carrying on with him, you know. With Logan. They've been at it for months.'

Chris Rushton's interest quickened a little, despite himself. 'This is a very serious accusation to make, Darcy. And unless you think it has any bearing on Mr Logan's death, you shouldn't really—'

'She's well capable of violence, Tamsin Phillips is. Well capable of killing, when she's roused.'

'Really? Well, my advice to you—'

'You don't believe me, do you? Well let me tell you, years ago, she did this to me!' He leapt from his chair and pulled his shirt up with both hands, until it almost obscured his excited face.

But it wasn't Darcy Simpson's face that DI Rushton and the rest of the people in the CID section at that moment were looking at. It was the livid purple knife scar extending from the centre of his chest to the left side of his abdomen.

Ten

D aniel Price enjoyed the Rotary lunch. He was quite surprised how much he enjoyed it. He had tried to analyse his feelings, and decided that he enjoyed his double life, enjoyed making this innocent part of it as convincing as possible. There was a certain satisfaction in persuading people that you were a splendid chap, when all the time you knew that you weren't.

Daniel had set up his own business at thirty, a successful computer software firm. It was prosperous enough, even in these competitive times. Not quite as prosperous as most people in the Rotary thought, of course. But then they weren't to know that their affable companion at the lunches and other Rotary functions had another and more lucrative source of income. They merely assumed from his open-handedness and lavish lifestyle that Price Computer Supplies must be doing very well indeed.

Daniel downed a very acceptable raspberry pavlova in the dining room of the White Hart and contributed his share to the pleasant hubbub of conversation and laughter in the long, low-ceilinged room. Most of the others went quickly away after coffee to their various workplaces, but Daniel stayed for a few minutes to chat to the few who remained. When he was asked to help with the latest project to raise funds for disabled children, he shook his head regretfully and explained that he was far too busy to offer practical assistance. But he made a generous donation from his own pocket 'to get the ball rolling'.

The treasurer for the project was absurdly grateful. Daniel smiled quietly as he went out to his Mercedes. He wondered what the reaction would be if the worthy man knew where that money had come from.

He would go back to the offices of Price Computer Supplies later in the afternoon. But first he had another piece of work to undertake, a workforce of an entirely different sort to motivate. He moved the rear-view mirror in the Mercedes for a moment to check his appearance, ensuring that his dark, thick, wavy hair was perfectly in place.

He was a vain man at times, he thought, recognizing the weakness in himself without any feeling of guilt. Instead of guilt, he allowed a small smile of satisfaction to steal for a moment over his handsome, sallow features. It was a face, he decided, designed for impassivity and concealment, a face well fitted for deception. That was just as well.

The engine of the big Mercedes purred into life. Daniel Price eased the maroon saloon out of the White Hart car park and away towards that other, secret life.

The full post-mortem report on Peter Logan offered little that was new.

It confirmed that the headmaster had almost certainly been killed in the park where the body was found. Marks in the sparse grass under the trees had suggested to the SOCO team that the body had probably been moved no more than two metres after it had fallen, to place it under the cover of the copse of trees at the site. The PM reinforced this view. There were no marks on the corpse to suggest that it had been carried about after death.

'It looks as if he arranged to meet his killer in the park,' said DI Rushton.

'Or was taken there at gunpoint,' said Lambert, anxious to keep as open a mind as possible until he knew more. 'Is there anything more about time of death in the report?'

Rushton looked at the details he was transferring from

the printed page on to his computer. 'Nothing very precise. The body was lying in that copse for around twenty-four hours before it was found. "The evening of Monday 28th September" is obviously as far as they would go in court. Stomach contents aren't as helpful as they might be, since he'd had nothing substantial since lunch at twelve thirty that day. Just tea and biscuits about four thirty to five, along with others at the conference in Birmingham. Pathology and forensic incline towards death early in the evening rather than late, though they wouldn't be happy to be definite about that in court.'

Bert Hook nodded. 'He couldn't have died before eight. It was probably some time between eight and half past eight. He left Birmingham University campus at ten to seven that evening.'

Rushton entered this latest fact on to his files. Lambert said to Hook, 'Did you find out anything else about his behaviour on the day of his death?'

'Only that he didn't seem at all nervous or distracted. He gave what everyone seems to think was an excellent address about secondary education generally and his school in particular, answered questions, led a discussion group in the afternoon, and was generally bright and cheerful all day. He was seen to make one phone call on his mobile, after lunch.'

'Which no one interviewed so far has admitted receiving,' said Rushton, who had checked the team files as soon as Hook had come back from Birmingham with his report.

'Weapon?' said Lambert.

Rushton shook his head dolefully. 'They couldn't even be precise about that. They haven't found the bullet. They're confident that a silencer was attached, and they've got a reasonable picture of the point of entry. They think there's a fair chance they could tie it up with the murder weapon, if we ever find one. From the extent of the damage to the

74

skull, they think a Smith and Wesson pistol is the most likely instrument.'

'Anything turned up yet from the preliminary interviews at the school?'

Rushton was pleased with this question. It was a proper build-up for the one unusual bit of information, which was going to come from him. 'Nothing much yet. One teacher has been mentioned by someone else, though. Singled out for special attention, as you might say.'

He told them about Darcy Simpson's visit, about his dramatic display of the chest scars, stemming, as he claimed, from an attack by a teacher at Greenwood School, Tamsin Phillips.

'Simpson isn't the most reliable sort of informant. Possibly on drugs; almost certainly psychologically disturbed, I should think. But we checked out his story with Thames Valley Police, where the incident took place. It seems to be substantially true. Apparently she stabbed him three times with a kitchen knife.'

'When was this?'

'Five years ago. They'd been living together. It seems to have been in a fit of jealous rage, when he wanted to end the relationship.' Chris Rushton's mouth wrinkled with distaste at the thought of such lack of control; his own marital break-up had been much more civilized.

'So Ms Phillips has a criminal record.'

'No. She got off with a caution. Darcy Simpson refused to bring charges and the CPS wouldn't take it on without his co-operation. She agreed to a course of psychiatric treatment, so I suppose they thought they hadn't much chance of a custodial sentence.' Rushton's face creased with contempt in the policeman's conditioned reaction to any mention of psychiatry.

'Did Phillips make any mention of the incident in her interview at the school?'

'No. Simpson only came in here after she'd given her

statement.' He flashed the page up on the screen. 'This is absolutely routine: she says she didn't know Logan well; found him an excellent headmaster; had no idea who could possibly wish to kill him. No one's been back to her since Simpson came in here. I rather thought you'd like to follow it up yourself, sir.'

Lambert nodded and grinned. 'I'll take Bert with me to protect me against kitchen knives.'

'There's one other thing Simpson said about Ms Phillips. He claimed she'd been having an affair with her late head-master.'

Daniel Price drove his car round the ground floor of the multi-storey car park, checking that he was unobserved, and then eased it down the driveway to the basement.

There was little daylight down here. In the evening, the druggies and drop-outs would congregate here, but there were only two pathetic figures now, sitting with their backs against the concrete wall at the far end of the basement; Daniel kept well clear of them. The place smelt dank and foetid, with that strange combination of stale urine and the strong disinfectant the authorities used to try to cleanse the place.

He found the man he wanted when the invisible figure lit a cigarette, the match rasping into brief illumination, then leaving the tip of the cigarette glowing red in the gloom by the wall. The tiny red tip was all Price could see until he was very close to the man. He did not stand opposite him, but went and stood beside him, so that both of them were in the deepest shadow against the wall, observant of any other entry into this daunting place.

They stood thus for ten seconds before Price said, 'You'd better tell me what you want quickly. There's no point in hanging about here longer than we have to.'

'The usual horse and coke. More ecstasy. They're always after that. And Rohypnol. The demand for that keeps going up.'

The date-rape drug. The demand was going up everywhere, not just here. The man with the cigarette chuckled in the near-darkness, eliciting an answering snigger from Price. It was a mirthless, chilling exchange. But there was no one in this depressing place to hear them. Daniel said, 'I'll get you whatever I can. Rohypnol's difficult. The rest you'll have.'

A grunt of approval. Then the man waited, knowing there would be more. Price could have taken his order without risking a meeting. There must be more to be said. This man was below Price in the industry's obscure chain of command, was waiting to hear what his supplier would have to say. He couldn't see how it could be anything good for him.

Daniel let him have another nervous pull on the cigarette before he spoke, watching the end glow more brightly for a couple of seconds in the gloom. Then he said, 'You need to increase your turnover. If you sell more, I can get it cheaper. I can pass the saving on to you.'

Try the positive approach first: appeal to greed. You should only threaten if you needed to. But Daniel Price was beginning to realize that he rather enjoyed offering threats.

'It's – it's not easy.' The red spot burned bright again from another nervous pull.

'The demand's there, if you look for it. That's the advantage of what we sell, the market can always be extended.' Another chuckle, this time at the vulnerability of human nature. Only Daniel tittered this time.

The man in front of him said, 'You have to be careful. Watch who you're talking to.'

He was feebly stating the obvious, not offering a reason for his failure to sell more, and both of them knew it. He threw his cigarette half-smoked on to the concrete beneath their feet, then stamped on it.

Daniel could catch the panic on the narrow features, now that his eyes had adjusted to the half-light. He thought he could also smell fear on the man, though it was difficult to be certain in this foetid place. He exulted in his power to instil fear. This is how official torturers must have felt; this must have been what made men join the Gestapo. He had read a lot about war crimes, and Stalin's secret police. He said abruptly, 'How's trade going at the school?'

'We need to be careful there. Now that the Head's been killed, the place is swarming with police.' It was perfectly true. So why did it fall from his lips sounding like a feeble excuse?

'Of course we have to be careful. Always. Not just now. But you haven't answered my question.'

'Well, the trade's going all right. I'm having to replace two people who've left at eighteen and gone on to other places.'

'But you'll have done that, by now. You'll have been thinking ahead, someone with your efficiency.' Price let his contempt roll over the last phrase.

'Yes. I've got one new pusher already in place.' He thought for a moment of Mark Lindsay, that gangling boy he had recruited, and was glad that Daniel Price was not able to inspect him. 'I'm shifting plenty of pot, and the fifth and sixth-formers are looking for ecstasy and—'

'Not much profit in cannabis, not nowadays. You want to get them on horse and coke, whenever you can.'

Heroin and cocaine, the two staples of the drug barons, the two substances that offered most profit to the suppliers and most grief to the users, in the end. The man beside Price said, 'Yeah, I know that, but it takes time. They're only kids, you know.'

'You can't afford to think like that!' said Price sharply. 'We're below the national average, you know, with the kids.' He enjoyed quoting statistics, just as though this was as legitimate a business as his computer software. 'One in every seven kids in the eleven to fifteen age-range has taken drugs in the last month. Your figures are well down on that, you know.'

'Are they? Well, we're not in the middle of a big city in Cheltenham, and Greenwood Comprehensive is a good school.

Perhaps we shouldn't expect to sell as much there as—'

'Statistics don't lie.' Daniel was well aware of Disraeli's view on that, but he knew his listener wasn't. 'Three per cent of sixteen-year-olds have tried heroin. So the market's sitting there waiting to be exploited. You're not shifting any horse in the school, at the moment.'

'All right. I'll do my best.'

'But discreetly, of course.' Daniel was always prepared to have the best of both worlds.

'Yes. As I say, the school is swarming with police at the moment, so it might pay us to lie low for a bit.'

'Us? You, I think you mean. I don't propose ever to set foot in the place.'

'No. Well, me, then. I think I'd better lie low. Keep away from Greenwood for a while. I could try to sell more at Shakers.'

'Your call, sunshine. But the coppers in Greenwood at present aren't Drugs Squad. They'll be gone in a day or two, leaving the field clear for a resourceful businessman like you. Just remember that the big boys above us will want to see returns. I wouldn't like you to attract their attention for the wrong reasons.'

The man wished now that he hadn't ground out the cigarette when there was still smoking left in it. He desperately needed to fill his lungs with smoke. The sinister, anonymous big men of the drugs trade didn't just make you redundant if your sales fell. They were likely to eliminate you, in case you knew things you shouldn't. This man knew nothing about the chain above Price, wanted to shout through the great echoing cave of the car park that he did not. Instead, he said, 'Well, if that's all, I'll be off then.'

'That's all. For the moment. I've enjoyed our little meeting! It's a great help when you get things clear, isn't it? I think you'd better stay here though, for a few minutes. Wouldn't do for us to be seen departing at the same time, would it? I'll go first, I think.'

Daniel Price strolled unhurriedly to his car, enjoying the man's petrified obedience. He revved the Mercedes loudly, knowing its engine would reverberate like thunder in the confined space of that concrete basement. He turned the car not towards the exit, but towards the man he had just left, switching full headlights for a moment on to the slight, surprisingly tidy figure, catching the glint of his gold earring, enjoying the terror in the face as the man threw his hand up against the harsh white dazzle of the undipped bulbs.

He revved the engine threateningly again, moved the car forward a little, as though contemplating crushing the defenceless body against the wall, and then swung abruptly away, up towards the exit and the daylight.

He was back in his office at Price Computer Supplies within ten minutes, full of bonhomie after a Rotary lunch which had stretched pleasantly into the afternoon.

Eleven

Tamsin Phillips did not look like a woman who would take a knife to a man.

She had black wavy hair, cut short around an oval face, a retroussé nose, and large, dark eyes. The staff files showed that she was now thirty-three: she looked and dressed a little younger than that.

Hook had asked when he made the appointment that she should stay behind after the school day. She readily agreed, voicing the thought he had left unspoken that this would give them rather more privacy. She now led superintendent and sergeant through a deserted classroom and into a small room with a single window behind it. 'We call this our History Resources Room,' she said, gesturing vaguely towards the books on one wall and the rolled maps and document facsimiles leaning against another. 'It gives us a room where we can prepare lessons and mark essays on our own.'

'History is your main subject?' said Lambert. You had to start somewhere.

'History and Business Studies, nowadays. History is what I was appointed for, but Business Studies is the great bandwagon subject nowadays, and Peter asked me to mug it up a bit.'

'That would be Peter Logan?' queried Hook, who had produced his notebook.

'Yes. He was always pretty relaxed, you see, when we weren't in front of children or parents.'

If she thought she had made a gaffe with the first name,

she didn't show it. But schools were much more informal nowadays; Logan had probably actually encouraged the use of his forename. Perhaps she was anxious to get away from the issue, for she went on quickly, 'Some say Business Studies is no more than a mish-mash of other subjects, without any intellectual backbone of its own.'

'And what would *you* say, Ms Phillips?' asked Lambert dryly.

'Oh, I couldn't possibly comment.' She grinned at her irony, looking suddenly very pretty. 'And it's Tamsin. Or Miss Phillips, if we have to be formal. Ms is all right in writing, but I hate the sound in speech.'

'You've already spoken to one of our officers.'

'Yesterday. Can't remember the name, but she struck me as very efficient. Nice to see young women making their way in the modern police service.'

She seemed to be enjoying fencing with them. Lambert found himself suddenly far more annoyed with her than he should have been. 'We're here to follow up certain matters arising from what you said. It appears that you may not have been completely honest in your statement. Hardly honest at all, if we accept certain information which has been brought to us.'

'And do you accept that information?'

'Not yet. We're here to investigate just how reliable it might be. And how reliable your initial statement was. Perhaps I should remind you that this is a murder inquiry. Any attempt to obstruct the course of the investigation would be regarded very seriously by a court of law.' His manner was stiff, but bristling with menace. He found himself using the formality of the words of warning to control his own anger.

'You've been talking to Darcy.'

'We don't normally reveal our sources of information. But yes, Mr Simpson came into the station to talk to us.'

'I'll bet he did!'

'Mr Simpson was doing no more than his duty as a citizen,

if he had information which he thought might be relevant to a murder inquiry.'

'Oh, yes, he'd enjoy that, Darcy would. Bet he couldn't wait to get to you. Impressed you as a perfectly balanced individual, did he?'

'Neither Sergeant Hook nor I have seen Mr Simpson. He spoke to Inspector Rushton at Oldford CID.'

'And your Inspector said Darcy Simpson was a sober citizen doing his duty, did he? I bet he did.'

'Miss Phillips, we are not at this moment concerned with the mental stability of our informant. It is our duty to check out the truth or otherwise of what he has told us. That, in this case, happens also to mean that we are checking out the truth of what you said to a member of our murder team last night.'

'All right. I was economical with the truth, I suppose. I didn't see why my private life should be dragged into the spotlight.'

'So you lied.'

'I concealed things, yes.'

'By lying.' Lambert was anxious to have this seemingly composed young woman on the back foot when they got to the heart of this exchange.

'Is it important how I protected myself?'

'I think it is, yes. At best you have wasted police time in a murder investigation. At worst, you have deliberately given false information in an attempt to divert suspicion away from yourself. Either way, you should realize that it's very serious. You should also take stock of your position at this moment. I should warn you that you would be foolish in the extreme to attempt further lies in the next few minutes.'

I must be getting older and nastier, thought Lambert: I'm quite enjoying this. And Tamsin Phillips was at last looking ruffled. She said sulkily, 'I told you, I was merely trying to keep my private life to myself. You'd better ask me whatever you want to now.'

'Is it true that you have a history of physical violence? That you were very lucky not to face a charge which might well have brought you a custodial sentence?'

She sighed theatrically. 'Good old Darcy! Showed you his scars, did he? Yes, it's true enough. I was younger and sillier, then. I stabbed him all right. Three times. Nearly killed the bugger! Perhaps I should have done!' She was suddenly exultant, her face flushed with the memory of her violence, her dark hair agitated by the animated movements of her head.

'According to the records of the Thames Valley Police, it seems that it was only Darcy Simpson's refusal to bring charges which saved you from a court appearance and a probable custodial sentence.'

'I'd never have gone to prison. I was high on LSD, and my psych. would have said I was too unstable to be convicted! What I can't fathom now is why I took such exception to being ditched by a weirdo like Darcy Simpson.'

There was a heavy silence in the cramped little room, whilst the CID men let the enormity of her error sink in. Lambert's instinctive attempt to rattle her had succeeded. At length he said, 'Still unstable, are you, Miss Phillips? Unstable enough to blow a man's head away with a pistol, perhaps?'

She started from her chair, and Hook for a moment thought she was going to strike Lambert, who moved not an inch. Then she sank back and said in what was almost a whisper, 'I didn't kill Peter Logan.'

'Then presumably you would like to see whoever did kill him brought to justice. Your actions so far have scarcely contributed to that.'

She raised both hands to her face, then pulled them swiftly away, as if she felt her cheeks burning her fingers. Then she said sullenly, 'You'd better ask me whatever questions you wish.'

'And you in turn should not only answer truthfully, but also offer us any other information or opinions you think might be useful in a murder inquiry. What was your relationship with Peter Logan?'

'He was an excellent head teacher. A good leader, with lots of energy and ideas. I'm sure other people will—'

'And what was your personal relationship with him?'

The face which had recently flushed was whitening now, its pallor accentuated by the black hair which framed it. 'Darcy Simpson told you about this, didn't he?'

'I'm interested in what *you* have to tell us. In what you held back from us last night.'

'All right.' She sat silently for a moment, with her hands together on her lap. Lambert stared hard into her face; he would have given much to know whether she was gathering herself for what she had to reveal or whether she was calculating what she could still hold back. 'Peter and I had an affair.'

'Had? It was over at the time of his death?'

Again a tiny pause. 'Were having, I should say. We were still lovers at the time of his death.' Tears gushed in a flood from those large, dark eyes, seeming to startle her as much as them by their suddenness. Lambert offered no words of consolation, just as he had stared hard into her face during her earlier distress, knowing how the absence of the usual social niceties unnerved those who were not used to the business of interrogation.

'How long had this been going on?'

'Seven months. We'd been lovers for the last six.' No hesitation this time, and the precision of one involved in a serious affair of the heart.

'How serious was it?'

A flash of irritation in the oval face at the deliberate banality of his question. 'What is serious? Do you want me to give you the intensity on a scale of one to ten?' She stared challengingly into the unblinking grey eyes, but Lambert watched and waited, saying nothing. Eventually, she dropped her gaze to the scarred table between them and said bleakly, 'We felt a lot for each other.'

85

'How public was this relationship?'

'Very private. We had to be discreet. For one thing, Peter had two children in the school, until July. He still has one. I taught Catriona for her History GCSE.' She allowed herself a small smile at the strangeness of that, and even that tiny relaxation lit up her face. It was easy to see why that strange young man Darcy Simpson had clung to his memory of her.

'Did Mrs Logan know about it?'

'No.' The monosyllable came almost too quickly on the heels of the question. 'I'm sure she didn't. We weren't planning divorce or anything like that. It was intense but – but . . .'

'Short-term?' Lambert helped her out for once when she was lost for a word.

'No.' Again the swift denial, this time on a note of outrage. Perhaps she heard that note herself, for she lowered her voice as she went on. 'We cared a lot for each other, but Peter had a family, and I didn't want to disrupt that any more than he did.'

There was a hint of desperation as she spoke, as if she was trying to convince herself as well as her hearers of what she said. The experienced CID men in front of her had heard this sort of tale a hundred times before. They wondered what the man in the case would have said. That old problem with a murder case: the victim who can never speak for himself.

Lambert said, 'You say you were discreet about this. If this liaison went on for seven months, people will know about it, however cautious you think you've been.'

She looked for a moment as if she would deny the possibility, then shook her head ruefully. 'You're probably right. One or two people in the school probably twigged what was going on. Have they been talking about it?'

Lambert ignored that. Instead, he said, 'Darcy Simpson seemed to know all about your affair.'

'He did. He's obsessed with me.'

'Despite what you did to him?'

'Yes. If anything, it seemed to increase his hang-up. He was ditching me at the time, but he came out of hospital convinced I was the one for him. He said what I had done showed the depth of my passion. He took a job here when I moved to Cheltenham. He rings me up, sometimes three or four times a week. I've seen him following me in the town. I could have him for stalking, if I wanted to.'

'But as you nearly killed him once, you won't, Miss Phillips. If Darcy Simpson knows about your affair with Peter Logan, be assured that other people will also know. You were very foolish to try to keep it from us.'

'I accept that, now.' She looked suddenly very weary. 'I followed my first instincts to keep our relationship secret. I'd been secretive for so long that I suppose it was a habit. Well, you know now, and I recognize that I was foolish. Is there anything else?'

'Yes. Did you kill Peter Logan?'

Even Hook was surprised by the sudden aggression of the question. But Lambert had decided by now that sympathy was not the way to deal with Tamsin Phillips.

She looked furious for a moment. But all she said was a thin-lipped, 'No. Of course I didn't.'

'And have you any idea who did?'

'No. I've thought of nothing else since we were given the news yesterday morning, but I haven't the faintest idea. I'd certainly tell you if I had.'

'When did you last see Mr Logan?'

'In school. On the Friday before he died.' Again she scarcely opened her mouth. It seemed as if each syllable had to be forced out.

'And when were you last alone with him?'

A tiny pause. Her hands clasped and unclasped, but were perfectly still as she said, 'On the Wednesday night before that. Five days before he died.'

Lambert's voice became softer, almost sympathetic for the first time, as he said, 'Peter Logan was seen leaving the

Birmingham University campus at ten to seven on Monday evening. We think he was back in Cheltenham by eight thirty at the latest. But Mrs Logan was not expecting him home until around eleven. Did he come to see you on the night he died?'

Her voice was very low as she responded to Lambert's quiet questioning. 'No. I told you, the last time I saw him was during a normal school day on the Friday before he died.'

'Then have you any idea where he intended to go on Monday night?' Lambert was almost apologetic in his tone, but both of them knew the importance of the question.

Several seconds seemed to pass before she said dully, 'No. I knew he was at the conference on Monday. I thought he would be going straight home.'

'It seems probable that he had arranged to meet someone that night. Someone who killed him. You can't even hazard a guess as to who that someone might be?'

'No. Peter didn't say anything to me about a meeting.'

They left her staring hard at the blank wall of the little room.

Hook had driven the police Mondeo through the school gates and on to the road outside them before he said, 'You went hard at her.'

'Yes. She annoyed me, Bert, though that's no excuse. But perhaps the fact that she'd been dishonest to start with earned her a little harshness.'

Hook smiled. He had known men harsher, in his time. He'd known men who'd reduced witnesses to tears much faster than had happened today, without getting as much out of them as John Lambert did in quieter ways. He said, 'She told us about her affair with Peter Logan readily enough, once you got to work on her. I'm beginning to get rather a different feeling about the private life of our late saintly headmaster.'

Lambert said nothing. He was wondering whether even now Tamsin Phillips had been wholly honest with them.

Twelve

Detective Sergeant Bert Hook made surprisingly good progress with Archie Weatherly, the seventy-year-old industrialist he was visiting because Weatherly was a governor of Greenwood Comprehensive School.

They were chalk and cheese these two, the consciously old-fashioned captain of industry and the slightly overweight CID man with his village bobby exterior. But Bert was a Barnardo's boy, who had met many wealthy patrons in his late adolescence in the home. He never minded being patronized by people like Weatherly. It put them off their guard, made them underestimate him, made them reveal things about themselves and other people which they didn't intend to reveal, sometimes didn't even realize they had revealed at all. Hook entered the huge office of the non-executive director of the building company and found himself brusquely directed to an upright chair in front of the big desk. He took it without irritation.

'I thought they might have sent someone of higher rank than a sergeant to interview a man who'd been a governor since the school was set up,' grumbled Weatherly.

'Big team. Fully deployed,' said Hook, gnomically but affably. 'Still, I expect Superintendent Lambert will want to speak to you later, if you can point us towards the murderer.'

'Can't do that. Can't really see why you want to speak to me anyway. I'm an industrialist, not a schooly.' Archie Weatherly dredged up a term from almost half a century earlier, when he had been a military man. He apparently saw no contradiction in the ideas that he had nothing to say but should nevertheless be interviewed by the top man in the case.

He now leaned forward confidentially towards Hook, smelling revoltingly of tobacco and aftershave, and said, 'We're even getting murders in Cheltenham now. If you ask me, it's another example of this random violence that's taking the country over.'

DS Hook restrained the comment that he wasn't asking him. 'There's been a lot of violence for a long time now, sir, even in Cheltenham. But very little of it is completely random. Most of it has a purpose, even if it's a criminal purpose.'

Weatherly frowned, then nodded slowly. 'You think he was mugged, do you? Well these young buggers are running out of control all right. Need a touch of the birch, if you ask me.'

Bert didn't. 'We're almost certain this wasn't a mugging, sir. Mr Logan's pockets didn't appear to have been touched. His death is much more likely to have been at the hands of someone who knew him.' Or someone hired by such a person: but Hook didn't want to trail such a complication across the brain processes of the man in front of him.

Weatherly slowly digested the thought that he might even have had contact with Logan's killer. He found it a surprisingly attractive idea. It brought a welcome excitement into what he was finding an increasingly dull life. 'See whatcha mean, Sergeant. Rum do, this. So you want me to suggest who might have killed young Logan.'

'We don't really expect that, sir. It would be remarkable if you could lead us straight to our killer.' More like bloody impossible, thought Bert. 'This is just a routine inquiry really; we're getting in touch with anyone who had contact with the murder victim, in the days before he died. There is no suggestion, of course, that you might have killed Mr Logan yourself.'

Weatherly guffawed at the absurdity of such a notion.

'But you might have noted some abnormality in the behaviour of the murder victim himself—'

'No. Can't say I did. Young Logan was full of himself and his school at the governors' meeting last week – as usual. Not that he didn't have things to boast about, you understand. Greenwood seems to be doing very well – for a school in the state system, of course.'

'—or some peculiarity in the attitude or actions of those around him,' concluded Bert Hook rather desperately.

Archie Weatherly digested this slowly, nodding as the full import of Hook's suggestion took root. For the first time since Hook had arrived in his office, he thought carefully. Like many a less exalted person, he felt the macabre glamour of that word murder, and wished to maintain a contact with the hunt, however tenuous. His brow furrowed, then lightened as a thought came to him. Bert Hook wished the criminal suspects he spent his life crossing swords with were as transparent as this ageing captain of industry. He prompted his man. 'Any ideas you have will be treated in the strictest confidence, of course.'

'Fenton. Stephen Fenton.'

Hook made a note of the name. When no further details emerged from the man behind the big desk, he said gently, 'Is Mr Fenton a member of the school staff, sir? We have a team of—'

'No, no, of course he isn't.' Weatherly shook his head as if he despaired of the modern police service. 'He's a governor of Greenwood School, like me. He was the Chairman for a couple of years. Made quite a good job of it, I believe.'

'And why would this give him a connection with the Headmaster's death?' asked Hook patiently.

Weatherly looked immensely conspiratorial. He leaned forward, though the size of his desk still kept him some eight feet away from Hook and made the movement a little ridiculous. 'Spoke to him a few days ago. Told him

91

he should become Chair of the Governors again. He turned me down flat!'

Weatherly sat back with the air of a man who has dropped a bombshell into a humdrum investigation. Hook waited for a moment to see whether the man would enlarge on Fenton's refusal, then said diffidently, 'And you think this might have some significance, sir?'

'Every significance, surely? Fellow turned me down flat on the phone. And I made it clear I could have fixed it for him.' He shook his head sadly; he was not used to men who turned down the chance of promotion, even in the arcane and unpaid world inhabited by school governors.

'Did Mr Fenton give you any reason for refusing to reassume the chair?' said Hook dutifully.

'No. Well, he said he had two children in the school and there could be a clash of interests if he was Chairman, that he didn't want to be seen to be favouring the progress of his own kids, but I'm sure that couldn't have been the real reason.'

Hook did not permit himself the sigh of frustration he felt so tempted to indulge. Men like Archie Weatherly did not take kindly to having their ideas dismissed. Instead, he took his leave politely, with the usual injunctions to Weatherly to get in touch if he had further relevant thoughts on this crime.

As he climbed into his car, he thought resignedly that his visit to Weatherly had been a waste of time, one of those many blind alleys which are inevitable in a murder investigation.

DS Bert Hook was for once quite wrong.

Collating the plethora of information which is gathered during the first days of a murder investigation is a taxing but generally rather dull administrative job. DI Chris Rushton was good at the work. He was not overawed by the welter of information from a large team, and his system of computer cross-referencing often threw up interesting connections which might otherwise have been overlooked.

And occasionally, but often enough to keep him excited, being back at headquarters in the CID at Oldford whilst his eccentric Superintendent was out and about put him in pole position, made him the first one to receive some unexpected gem of information.

The voice on the other end of the phone on the morning of Friday, the second of October, asked for Superintendent Lambert, the man in charge of the case. Chris concealed his irritation as he explained that John Lambert was out interviewing suspects in the case and that he was the Inspector collating all information. Once the initial scepticism at the other end of the phone had declined into mere surprise, the woman passed him on to her superior.

'Superintendent Johnston here. National Paedophile Unit, New Scotland Yard. I understand John Lambert isn't available.'

'Not at present, sir. He's out on the case. I can give him a message. It's DI Rushton here. I'm in charge of the collation of information on the Peter Logan murder.'

'Right. Important piece of information for you, then. Peter Logan rang the Paedophile Unit on the Friday before he died. Said he had reason to believe that a member of his staff was indulging in paedophilia.'

Chris Rushton gulped, like a newspaperman sensing a scoop. 'Did he give you a name?'

'No. He said he didn't think there was any immediate urgency because he'd no evidence the man was active with children in the school. It was a man, by the way: you'd be surprised how many women we've turned up in the last year. And it was a teacher, not a member of the ancillary staff. But that's the only help I can give you. Logan was due to speak to me again on Tuesday of this week. I wondered why he hadn't come back to me. Now I find he's dead.'

'And you think his death might be connected with this?'

There was a note of world-weary impatience in Johnston's voice as he said, 'Yes, of course I do. Paedophilia is big business now. If this man was part of a ring, they might well have silenced Logan to keep their activities secret.'

'And you've no idea which member of the teaching staff this might be? There are over fifty of them.'

'No. And I doubt whether anyone else knows. Logan implied he was keeping his thoughts strictly to himself within the school. That's understandable: you land yourself in all kinds of trouble if you accuse someone working in a school of paedophilia without being certain of your ground.'

'Right. I'll let Superintendent Lambert know immediately. I'm sure he'll liaise with you when he finds out more.'

When, not if, thought Chris Rushton. He wondered if he had just found the lead to the killer of Peter Logan.

The sitting room in Jane Logan's home, which had been littered with used cups and plates when they had been here last, was very tidy now. They were able to look through the window which had been curtained on Wednesday evening, down a long back garden where dahlias still blared their colours defiantly and bright blue Michaelmas daisies were mounds of early autumn colour.

Jane Logan looked as tidy as her surroundings. When Lambert apologized for disturbing her, she said, 'There's no need. You said you'd be back, and I've been given time off from my work until Monday.'

'You are a teacher yourself, I understand.'

'A little, yes. Just two evenings a week at the College of Technology. I teach mostly adults who are hoping to go on to higher education. I manage a flower shop during the day.'

Bert Hook said, 'The children must have been a great help to you.'

Jane Logan smiled. 'They were very supportive. Of each other as well as me. I've sent them back to their friends now. Catriona's back at Greenwood and Matt's gone back to university. He said he'd stay here, but I could see he was relieved to get away. It's an exciting time, your first weeks at university.'

'So you're on your own today.'

'Yes. It's better that way. To tell you the truth, I shall be quite relieved to get back to work on Monday.'

Lambert was studying her closely. He said, 'I'm afraid the body won't be released for burial for some time yet.'

She nodded, perfectly composed. 'That was explained to me by the coroner's officer. When you find who killed him, the defence has the right to request a second post-mortem. I've explained it all to the children. They were a little upset at first, but they saw the logic of it. It's not a problem.'

Lambert nodded, his eyes never leaving the face below the dark blonde hair. Then he said, 'I hope you will forgive us if we probe one or two sensitive areas this morning. I'm afraid it's our job to probe, in an attempt to get as full and rounded a picture of a murder victim as we can.'

She took this in, paused for a moment, then said with a smile, 'That won't be a problem. I gather from what you say that you haven't got what I believe is called a prime suspect as yet.'

Lambert gave her a small answering smile. She was as watchful and observant as he was, an opponent worthy of his steel. She might also be a murderess; he found the irrelevant thought intruding into his old-fashioned mind that the feminine term might no longer be politically acceptable.

He said, 'No, we haven't turned up an obvious suspect yet. You may know that three quarters of murders are committed within the immediate family. Once you move outside that close circle, things are usually more complex.'

She smiled. 'Then I trust on this occasion you are finding things more complex.' She put her hands on the arms of her armchair and leaned back a little, as if to show how much at ease she was in a situation which must be quite new to her. Her fair hair was perfectly groomed, her face lightly but skilfully made up to enhance the blueness of her eyes.

From her looks alone, she might have been widowed for three years, rather than three days.

Lambert said, 'Forgive the observation, but unless you are hiding it very skilfully, you do not seem to be riven with grief by this unexpected tragedy.'

There was a moment of electric silence, as if both Bert Hook and Jane Logan were checking the import of his quietly spoken words. Then the woman opposite him spoke as quietly as he had. 'In other circumstances, that would be impertinent. But you have already explained that these are not ordinary circumstances. I am glad my children are not here, and I would hope as little of this as possible reaches them.' She reached forward to the low table and took up the pot of coffee she had made for their visit, pouring three cups without a tremor, watching the movements of her arms as if their steadiness gave her particular pleasure.

She handed them the cups before she said, 'There is a difference between public and private life. The *Times* obituary is perfectly accurate, as far as it goes. But you must understand that it is possible for a man to be an outstanding head teacher while being much less effective as a husband and a father.'

'You're telling us that Mr Logan's home life was less successful than his professional one?'

'I'm trying to obey your opening injunction, to give you as full a picture of the life of a dead man as I can.' She sipped her coffee, and they sensed that she had keyed herself up for this, that her honesty was in some ways a relief for her, after keeping up the conventions in front of her children and others.

Lambert nodded. 'Thank you. How bad was the situation in this house, Mrs Logan?'

She took her time, organizing her mind to deliver thoughts she had rehearsed before they came. 'We married young, Peter and I, then grew apart rather than together. We've had a series of blazing rows over the years, but not many of them in front of the children.' She gave a bitter smile at herself. 'The conventional middle-class marriage breakdown, in fact. You tell yourselves you're staying together for the sake of the children, but that might be mere cowardice. And Peter would never have divorced me. His career wouldn't have allowed it. Over the years, I've come to detest that word "career".'

But it won't upset you any longer now, thought Lambert. You'll be free to do whatever you want, re-marry with anyone you choose. He said, 'Forgive me, but I need to ask this. Have either of you had other partners in the last few months?'

She had steeled herself for this, knowing that it must arrive, that it was a natural outcome of her earlier frankness. It was an effort nonetheless to keep her voice steady as she said, 'Peter had had a series of affairs over the years. He assured me that he always came home, so that was all right.' The contempt came flaring out on the last phrase.

'But it wasn't all right with *you*.'

'I suppose it wasn't, really. But I didn't want to scratch his eyes out any more. We existed in what I suppose you could call armed neutrality for most of the time. I'd got to the stage where I knew Peter would never be faithful but I no longer cared who he was currently bedding. We didn't have separate bedrooms or anything like that in this house. The children again, I suppose. When there was nothing better around, he gave me some attention.'

'This is where I have to probe. We must know the names of the woman or women who were currently enjoying your husband's attentions.'

She laughed at that: a single, mirthless peal. 'Delicately put, Superintendent. I like that: "currently enjoying his attentions". I suppose they were: he could be very charming, Peter, until you knew him as well as I did. And he had power, you know, these last few years; the great aphrodisiac, they tell me. It's probably true, and you could take Peter as a case study.'

'This must be very upsetting for you, Mrs Logan. I'm sorry to open old wounds, but I must have names, please.'

'I'm sorry, but I can't help you. I told you, his affairs had become a matter of indifference to me by the time of his death. I'd worked hard to arrive at that indifference.'

Lambert wondered if she was quite as detached about the matter as she protested herself to be. Perhaps, as she claimed, she knew nothing about Tamsin Phillips or any other woman. But she had just outlined the conditions for a crime of passion, with herself as murderer, if you looked at the situation from another viewpoint. He said, 'Would any woman involved with Peter be working in the school?'

She thought carefully for a moment. 'I should think it extremely likely. He does – did – work very hard in the school, and he hadn't many contacts outside it. He was a very good headmaster, with a touch of vision alongside huge organizing ability and energy. It was in the school context that his charisma was always most apparent and most potent. And in case you're thinking of asking, his tastes were strictly heterosexual. Peter was a traditionalist in that respect, at least.'

Lambert stared into her face for a moment, then reluctantly concluded that she was being honest about her ignorance of any relationships her husband had been conducting at the time of his death. He said, 'You said last time we were here that you were not expecting your husband home until ten thirty or eleven on Monday night.'

'Yes. That is the time he told me to expect him. I went to the gym in the evening. When he wasn't in by around eleven, I went to bed. I didn't realize until next morning that he had never arrived home.'

'We now think your husband was back in Cheltenham by eight thirty at the latest on that evening, though we cannot be precise about exactly when he died. He knew that the Birmingham conference would be over by six. Have you any idea why he told you to expect him back so much later?'

'I think you can deduce that from our conversation over the last ten minutes. My guess would be that he was planning to visit a woman. I've no evidence to support it, other than previous experience.'

'You will know by now that he was found in a park in the Leckhampton area. Does that location suggest anyone to you?'

'No. I've no interest in where his women lived.'

'There may be no woman involved, of course. Can you think of any other reason why he would have gone to the Leckhampton area?'

'No. The local paper seemed to imply that he might have been taken there against his will.'

'They were speculating, I'm afraid. But that is one possibility. Another is that he had arranged to meet someone in the park: someone who very possibly killed him there. A third possibility is the one I have just suggested: that he was on his way to meet someone in the area but was intercepted by the person who shot him.'

'I see. But I can't throw any light on the matter, however it happened.' For the first time, she seemed to give the matter little thought. She seemed anxious to close this area of discussion. Perhaps the detail of her husband's death was upsetting her more than she admitted.

'You've been very patient and understanding, Mrs Logan. I must probe one more sensitive area, I'm afraid. I said we were trying to build up a picture of your husband, who cannot speak for himself, and you have been very frank and helpful in adding detail to that picture. But people do not exist in isolation; we all live our lives in conjunction with those closest to us. I must therefore ask you about your own life. You have told us that your relationship with your husband was cool, even unhappy, for much of the time. In the light of that, have you struck up any serious relationship of your own?'

She stared for a moment into her now empty cup, trying to make sure that the anger was kept from her voice as she replied. 'I'm not sure that I would tell you if I had; it's none of your business. But the answer's no.'

Lambert refrained from telling her just why it was very much their business. She would recognize when they had gone, even if she did not do so now, that any lover of hers was a potential killer of Peter Logan's, a man who would have to be eliminated from the inquiry.

She saw them off from the door, as calmly as if they had been social callers rather than detectives probing the death of her husband. Her fair hair still framed her strong, attractive face as neatly as when they had arrived; her half-smile persisted as long as they could see her. She was still standing in the front doorway of the mock-Georgian house as they turned the corner and disappeared.

Hook concentrated upon his driving and did not speak. His Superintendent said eventually, 'So what did you make of Mrs Jane Logan, Bert?'

Hook negotiated a set of traffic lights before he said, 'Frank and helpful. More so than I would ever have expected, three days after her husband's death.'

'Yes. I can see Peter Logan a lot more clearly, now we've talked to her. She was largely unemotional, I thought, and pretty well-organized in what she said.'

Hook drove on for another half-mile, until Lambert decided he had said all he had to offer. Then Bert said, 'A little too helpful, too well-organized, perhaps? It made me wonder what she was holding back.'

Lambert grinned. 'Suspicious chaps, policemen.'

Thirteen

'I'm sorry to take you away from your duties again, Mrs Dean. Something urgent and serious has just come up.'

The blonde-haired Deputy Head was as flustered today as she had been calm two days earlier. The strain of running the school without Peter Logan, of taking on his directorial role as well as maintaining her own myriad administrative duties as Deputy Head, was telling on her. 'That's all right,' she said, more politely than she felt. 'Thank God it's Friday!'

'I apologize again, but I fear I'm here to add to your troubles.'

Lambert took her briefly through the phone call DI Rushton had received from the National Paedophile Unit at New Scotland Yard. 'This information must be treated as highly confidential, of course,' he concluded. 'Mr Logan had merely voiced a suspicion; it's possible there may be nothing in it. But it will have to be investigated.'

'Of course it will. We can't risk having anyone like that working with children. And if Peter Logan was suspicious of anyone, it wouldn't be without good reason. I reckon this means we've got a paedophile on the staff.' She sighed; just when she thought things at Greenwood were as chaotic as they could be, here was something to make things worse.

Lambert said quietly, 'This man may also be a murderer, or an accessory to murder. The Paedophile Unit thinks he's part of a ring. Some of these people are high-profile figures with a lot to lose. They wouldn't stop at hiring a professional killer to remove someone who could lay information against them.'

Pat Dean stared at him bleakly. 'You must do whatever you have to do, of course. All I ask is that you disturb the rhythm of the school as little as possible.' She smiled ruefully. 'This is the term when most of the really solid work is normally achieved. We could do without these distractions.'

'I appreciate that. I was hoping that Peter Logan would have discussed this with you, but he obviously didn't. So the problem is that we know only two things about the suspected paedophile: he is a member of your teaching staff, and he's male.'

'There are thirty-one male teachers at Greenwood.' She produced the figure without hesitation, then added dully, 'How do you propose to go about vetting thirty-one teachers?'

Lambert thought quickly. 'It's Friday. Mr Logan thought the man posed no immediate danger to the children in the school. We'll compile a list, then interview as many of them as we can in their homes over the weekend.'

She tried not to show the relief she felt on her face. 'That will certainly help to minimize the disruption to the routine of the school. You won't get through thirty-one over the weekend, though, will you? Is there any way we can agree a shortlist of leading suspects? For instance, I can't think that our Senior Master, who is fifty-three and has five children, is going to be a strong candidate for this.' She smiled at the thought, looking suddenly much more attractive under her tousled blonde hair. Then she wiped away her mirth in the face of the seriousness of the problem.

'Let's have the names of those who are male and single,' Lambert decided. 'I'm sure this isn't a politically correct way of going about things, but we've got to start somewhere, and statistics would support us in taking this line.'

Hook made some careful notes from the staff files. They went away with a list of five teachers, all of them youngish men. Four of them would be appalled by the notion the CID would bring into their innocent lives. If all five should prove blameless, then the trawl would need to spread more widely, and the life of Greenwood Comprehensive School would be even more savagely disrupted in the coming weeks.

It was early on that Friday evening that Mark Lindsay met the man who had drawn him into the drugs trade.

It wasn't a scheduled meeting. Mark was in a cubicle in the smaller gents' cloakroom at the far end of Shakers, checking his supplies, getting ready for the evening. This was the night when he was going to spread his wings, to start offering pot to people who were not at school with him, who were part of that still mysterious and exotic working world outside.

He was much more on edge than he had anticipated. He had intended to stay off the grass tonight, to keep his brain cool and clear for what he must now treat as a working evening. But he needed something to steady his nerves. After only a moment's hesitation, he was smoking one of the spliffs he had planned to keep for the weekend.

He felt better after it, as he had known he would. He could almost imagine he felt the confidence seeping back into his veins. A few months of successful selling, a few months of fat commissions from the mysterious men above him in the chain, and he'd be more than a match for those confident young men who were so loud at the bar, so successful with the girls.

He hadn't heard anyone come into the tiled room outside the cubicle. He flushed the loo and strode confidently out, preparing to check his hair in the mirror before venturing forth among the people he must now regard as his clientele.

The man who had recruited him was neither urinating nor washing his hands. He was standing perfectly still, with his arms by his side and a small smile on his face. He wore black trousers and shoes and a black top that was relieved only by a slash of scarlet colour at its centre. Mark wondered how long he had been there.

He waited for him to speak, but the man said nothing.

Against his will, seeming to have no control over his tongue, Mark faltered out words of his own to break the silence. 'I've sold quite a lot of grass this week.'

'In the school?'

'Yes. It's been a bit difficult because—'

'You'll need to extend your markets.'

'Yes. I'm planning to do that tonight. I think I'll be able—'

'Can't stand still in this game.' The man in black knew he shouldn't be pressurizing this young fool, that he was risking the success of his enterprise by pushing raw recruits into taking risks, but he couldn't see what choice he had. The words of Daniel Price in the shadows of that multi-storey car park rang still in his ears: 'Just remember that the big boys above us will want to see returns. I wouldn't like you to attract their attention for the wrong reasons.'

He looked at Mark Lindsay, saw him wilting before his eyes, and said, 'You'll need to get some of your customers at the school on to coke and horse. That's where the profit is.'

Mark hadn't been all that successful with the pot. He'd sold some, but that was to people who already used it, not new recruits to the game. And he'd had to let it go cheaper than his first asking price. He couldn't admit any of this to the man in black who watched him so closely. So he said, 'I know that the hard drugs are what bring in the big money. But I need time, see. You don't want me to take unnecessary risks, do you?'

He had hit a nerve there. The man didn't want any of his pushers to take unnecessary risks, but he had Daniel Price pressing him for expansion on his patch. It was an impossible situation. He said, 'I can get you good stuff. When your buyers find it's good, they'll be back for more. And they'll recommend you to others.'

'Yes. I can see that. But I thought I'd cut my teeth on the cannabis – build up a network of clients, like you said.'

The man couldn't recall just what he'd said. He only remembered press-ganging this stupid kid into his system, trying to extend his network in the school. He said, 'That makes sense. But you can't stand still in this game. There's others will want to come in and replace you, if you can't deliver.'

For a moment, Mark wanted to throw it all in and resign. Safe poverty seemed suddenly very attractive. But he knew from their last exchange that withdrawing wasn't an option. 'I'm hoping to get some new clients tonight. Maybe some of them will want the hard stuff.'

'You go carefully, me lad.' The warning came automatically, before the man in black could prevent himself. But probably young Lindsay was too nervous to recognize the contradiction. 'Tell them you can get coke and heroin, if they're interested. And I can supply you with a certain amount of Ecstasy and Rohypnol. Mention those: they're the ones to get the randy little sods interested.'

Mark wanted to say that he had only undertaken to deal in cannabis, that he would be getting out of his depth if he ventured upon hard drugs sales, that he was scared shitless about being involved as a dealer in them. But he knew he could say none of this to this man who frightened him so much amidst the echoing tiles of this small, deserted room.

He said, 'Thanks for the advice. I'm sure I can sell for you.'

Steve Fenton did not want to put the phone down and go back to the empty house.

He said, 'I had Archie Weatherly on at me the other day. Wanted me to become the Chairman of the Governors at Greenwood again. Said Peter needed someone at the helm who would curb his more expansive ideas. That was whilst he was still alive of course.'

'What did you say?'

'I told him I couldn't take it on again. I made the excuse that I had two children of my own in the school and things could get embarrassing.'

'And he accepted that?'

He could hear the anxiety in her voice. 'Yes, I think he took it at face value. He blusters a lot, Archie, and he's been a powerful man in his time, but he doesn't know much about schools.'

'It's important we keep a low profile.'

'I know that.' He wished he hadn't mentioned Weatherly now; he had only really done it to keep her on the phone. He found a safer topic. 'I still miss the kids, you know.'

'I know you do. Have you sorted out access?'

'Yes, I think so. Fairly amiably, as it turns out. I'm seeing them on Sunday. They're coming over here.'

'You're lucky still to have the house where they grew up. Most men are condemned to a round of zoos and grotty cinemas.'

It sounded as though she was rebuking him, as if she felt he should be counting his blessings instead of moaning. He knew it was no more than her instinctive attempt to cheer him up, but sometimes you wanted commiseration and sympathy, not reminders that you were luckier than some.

He came back to what they had begun with, to the topic which he knew dominated her thoughts at present. 'Anyway, they don't seem to know about us.' Both of them knew who 'they' were. The police, who seemed in their heightened imaginations to be swarming all over Cheltenham.

'And long may it remain so.'

'Yes. But I told you, even if they find out that we are in love with each other, there's nothing they can prove.' He kept saying this, because he had a feeling that they were going to find out, eventually.

'Perhaps not. But it's much better if we don't test that theory, Steve. They're going to wonder what else we've been concealing, if they find out we haven't told them about what we feel for each other.'

That was true enough. He had always had a feeling that the best form of defence was to tell as few lies as possible. But you couldn't turn the clock back now. He said hopelessly, 'I love you.'

It worked, in that he heard a little giggle at the other end of the phone. 'I love you too, you old softy. And I like to hear you say it. But it's much better that no one else knows, for the present. Good night, sweet prince, and flights of angels sing thee to thy rest!'

It was her usual affectionate, slightly mocking, farewell. For the first time, as he went back into the quiet kitchen, he wished she hadn't chosen her quote from *Hamlet*. That particular prince had come to a bad end.

Christine Lambert said, 'You look tired, John.' Her husband looked vulnerable and she wanted to mother him. It was a strange feeling, one she had only felt over the last year or two.

'I'm all right. This murder of the headmaster over at Cheltenham is going to take some cracking.'

'No pointers yet?'

'A few pointers, but in different directions. It's always the same in these cases. Unless there's an obvious suspect, unless you've made an arrest within twenty-four hours, you begin to turn over stones people would much rather you'd left undisturbed. You discover all kinds of things underneath them. Then you have to work out what is and what isn't relevant to this particular crime.'

'You'll sort it. You're good at these things. I know that, because the papers keep telling me it's so.' She enjoyed teasing him about his work, a thing she had never been able to do in the old days. Christine Lambert had had a mastectomy and a heart bypass in the last five years, and the tensions of those months had brought them much closer

107

together. She could not believe how anxious he had been for her; she sometimes thought he had been secretly rather surprised himself by the intensity of his feelings.

She realized now that he was giving full attention neither to the *Times* crossword on his knee nor to the television set which winked steadily in the corner of the room. He was preoccupied as usual with a puzzling case. But it was a healthy preoccupation, as far as murder could be healthy. He was more alert, more eager for life, than he had been last week, and his tiredness was probably the kind of satisfying fatigue that came from long hours of exacting labour.

'I'd like to solve this one, if it is to be my last murder,' he said suddenly. She knew that. She also noted the 'if'. This was bound to be his last case; it was time he accepted that. Was the core of him still stubbornly refusing to confront retirement, whilst he made all the conventional noises on the outside?

She said, 'Jacky's hoping to come over with the children tomorrow.'

'I'll probably be out, love. This case in Cheltenham, you see. Tell her I'll see her soon, if I miss her.'

He was like a dog with a bone, with a murder hunt to occupy him. Or a child with a new toy. But she wasn't going to change that particular sort of childishness now.

Long after John had fallen into an exhausted sleep, Christine Lambert was worrying about the years ahead.

Fourteen

S teve Fenton got only twenty minutes notice of the CID visit.

It was DS Hook, the voice on the phone said, the words slow and clear despite the rich Herefordshire accent. Sorry to bother him on a Saturday morning. It was just a matter of a few questions in connection with the investigation into the murder of Peter Logan. As Mr Fenton was a governor of Greenwood Comprehensive and a former Chairman of the Governors, he might have useful insights to offer. Hook's reassuring voice didn't exactly say that this was merely a matter of routine, but it implied as much.

It was only after Steve had put the phone down that he began to get nervous.

He was beset by an overwhelming need to occupy himself in physical action. He got the vacuum cleaner out and ran it over a carpet which did not need it; wiped the top of the units in an already tidy kitchen; behaved, he thought wryly, like a young wife expecting her mother-in-law.

They came very promptly at ten o'clock. The stolid detective sergeant he identified immediately as the owner of the local accent. The superintendent was a taller man with grey eyes which seemed to look into everything and see more than they should. Steve took them into his unused dining room and sat them down on upright chairs on the other side of the table from him. Even as they took the chairs he offered them, he found himself wishing he had seated them less formally in the sitting room, but it was too late for that now.

'I'm willing to give all the help I can, of course. This is a terrible business. But I'm afraid I haven't anything very useful to offer you.' Steve said it nervously, before they had even properly seated themselves, and regretted the banality of it immediately.

Lambert did not react to the disclaimer, did not even acknowledge it. 'You used to be Chairman of the Greenwood Governors, Mr Fenton. What kind of a man would you say Peter Logan was?'

Steve had rehearsed many scenarios in his mind over the last few days, but not this immediate directness, without any of the normal conversational preambles. 'Well, I only saw him in a professional context, of course. He seemed to me a very effective headmaster, and the results of his work are there for all to see.'

'What was your own relationship with him?' Those grey, unblinking eyes seemed to reinforce the directness of the approach.

Steve tried to seem as open and uncomplicated in his reply. 'We got on very well. I'm not an educationist, but I listened and learned. What Peter said usually made sense, and I saw my job as encouraging the governors of his school to provide the necessary backing. I like to think we made an effective partnership.'

'So why did you resign?'

'Personal reasons. Nothing to do with what has happened to Peter now.' The man had taken him by surprise. Steve felt that he should not have answered so huffily, that he was making more of the resignation than he should have, drawing attention to the matter.

'Mr Fenton, we are just trying to build up a picture of a man who has been brutally killed. You're helping us quite voluntarily: I can't insist that you answer, but I'd prefer to make up my own mind on what's relevant.'

'I had a business to run. Still have. A small engineering firm. We only employ ten people, so I need to be hands-on.'

'I see. But you felt able to accept the chairmanship in the first place?'

Steve wished he hadn't prevaricated. It was making him seem evasive when he'd really no need to be. The chairmanship of the governors wasn't really all that time-consuming: he wondered how much these men knew about it. 'I'd done my stint. Been Chair for over two years. I felt my business was suffering a little. And I've children in the school. There could have been a clash of interests.' He wished he'd used that argument to start with; it sounded more convincing in his own ears when he produced it now.

'So there was nothing more personal than that involved? There were no arguments between you and Mr Logan?'

'No. Peter and I got on very well.' He forced himself to look into those grey eyes which studied him so relentlessly, trying but failing to think of a little quip which might lighten the atmosphere.

'And that was still the case at the time of his death?'

He wondered who these men had been talking to, whether they treated everyone as if they had been an enemy of the dead man. 'Yes. Peter and I still had a very good professional relationship. We didn't see quite as much of each other after I ceased to be Chairman, but we—'

'Forgive me, but you have again laid stress on that word "professional". I am interested in more personal relationships.'

How sharp the man was! And how much did he know? Steve felt himself floundering. 'We got on well enough. I don't suppose we had a lot in common, outside our interest in the school. And the school was Peter's life, of course. He put in long hours—'

'So you didn't associate much socially?'

'No. We probably hadn't a lot in common, as I say.'

'Though you both had children in the school, and a common interest in the excellent education it was providing.' Lambert nodded a couple of times, inviting Steve to comment,

111

but this time he had the sense to keep his lips tightly shut. 'Would you say that Mr Logan had a happy home life?'

Steve was stiff with caution by now. 'I've no reason to think he didn't.'

'I speak in confidence, of course, but I think I can tell you that Mrs Logan intimated that in her view Mr Logan was a better headmaster than he was a husband.'

'That – that is surprising, but it may well have been so. I told you, we didn't associate much outside the school.'

'So you would hardly know Mrs Logan?'

'I've met her, at school functions.'

'That's hardly what I asked.'

'I've met her a few times, with Peter. She seems a very pleasant woman. She manages a florist's in the town, I'm told, but I've never been into the shop. And I think she teaches part-time at the College of Technology.'

Steve resolutely refused to elaborate in the long pause which followed. He had given up trying to look into those grey eyes, which seemed to peer into his very soul. He began to study a scratch on the surface of his dining table which he had never noticed before.

Eventually, Lambert said quietly, 'Where were you on Monday evening, Mr Fenton?'

'Here. From six thirty onwards.' His answer had come too quickly on the heels of the question, without any pause at all. He knew it as he spoke; told himself desperately that they couldn't make anything out of it.

'Was anyone with you for all or part of the evening?'

'No.' He'd waited a little longer before he answered this time. 'There's no reason why there should be, is there? I'm divorced. I live alone.'

'Indeed. It would have been useful from our point of view if someone had been with you, that's all.'

He hadn't said why he'd asked, thought Steve. The bugger was enjoying letting him work it out for himself, seeing him suffer. Well, he wasn't going to add any more. He had learned this morning that adding to your answers only made things worse, when you were lying.'

He looked up. Lambert was still studying his every tiny reaction with that steady, unembarrassed stare. 'Have you any idea who killed Peter Logan, Mr Fenton?'

'None whatsoever.'

'Do you know anyone who had a reason to dislike him?'

'No. I told you. He was highly successful in what he did.'

'Indeed you did tell us that. More than once. But success does not always make people likeable, does it?'

'I suppose not.'

'Did you ever hear that Mr Logan was something of a philanderer?'

What an old-fashioned word, thought Steve. He'd heard Logan called several things, had used some of the words himself, but never that one. He said stiffly, 'I didn't listen to gossip.'

'An admirable policy. But you can't help hearing things, sometimes. And, unlike you, he wasn't a free agent in these things.'

Steve almost blurted out a response he would immediately have regretted. This man was baiting him: he realized that now. No doubt they used anger to make people reveal things. Well, it wouldn't work with him. 'No. He was on the surface a happily married man. He'd a lot to lose. People expect a headmaster to be a pillar of respectability.'

'So he would have wanted to be secretive about any affair he conducted. But you don't know of any such clandestine association?'

'No. Well, I heard the odd rumour. But I told you, I didn't listen to gossip.'

'A pity, that, from our point of view. It means you probably have no idea whom he might have been planning to meet on the night he died.'

'No. I can't help you there.'

113

'Do you know where Mrs Logan was on that night?'

Steve seemed suddenly to have lost all his breath, like a boxer struck without warning below the belt. He wondered if his face showed how shaken he was. He tried to keep his voice steady as he said, 'No, of course I don't. Why do you want to know?'

The long, lined face on the other side of the table smiled for the first time in many minutes, amused by his naivety. 'Routine, Mr Fenton. The spouse is always a leading suspect in a murder case, until she's cleared. So far we haven't been able to establish exactly where Mrs Logan was on Monday night. It would have been useful if you could have helped us and her. But it was a foolish question really. Because as you say, you hardly know the lady.'

'No. My gut feeling is that she had nothing to do with her husband's death.'

'I see. Well, Sergeant Hook can hardly record gut feelings in his notes. He has to stick to facts, you see. And I've no doubt he's recorded that you didn't know Mr Logan very well, that you know his wife even less well, that you've no idea whom he might have been sleeping with at the time of his death. All negatives, but all no doubt very useful in their own way. All contributing to a fuller picture, when we put them together with what other people have to tell us.'

'Yes. I'm sorry I haven't been able to be more helpful.'

'Oh, it may be that you've been more helpful than you think at this moment, when we review the whole of our knowledge rather than the parts. I should remind you before we leave that if anything occurs to you which you think might be significant in the investigation, it is your duty to get in touch with us immediately. But no doubt you would wish to do that anyway!'

Almost before he had realized it, they had gone. It was a bright, pleasant autumn day outside, but Steve found his torso clammy with perspiration beneath his shirt.

It was a good five minutes before he recovered enough to go to the phone.

Mark Lindsay's mother wanted to know why he was going out. It seemed to him that he had to lie to everyone these days.

Saturday the third of October was one of those still, perfect autumn mornings, when the sun warmed the green land around Cheltenham after a cool start to the day, but Mark scarcely noticed the weather. His mind was teeming with too many other things and it even seemed hard work to turn the pedals of his bike.

Drugs trading wasn't proving the straightforward money-winner he had anticipated. And so far he didn't seem to be collecting the girls, which had been the object of the exercise. Indeed, one of the nicer girls from school, a fresh-faced blonde about whom he'd had some steamy erotic fantasies, had actually gone out of her way to come and talk to him in the club on the previous night, and he'd had to snub her. He hadn't meant to, but his social skills weren't up to turning a girl away without giving offence.

He'd had to get rid of her, because his supplier's ultimatum that he must shift more drugs was still strong in his mind, and he hadn't dared to forsake the opportunities of selling to talk to this friendly and delectable girl. Teething troubles, he told himself unconvincingly, as he rode his bike away from the town centre. In a few months, he'd have all the girls he could handle.

The man he now thought of as 'the man in black' was there before him. In fact, he wore Levi denims and a roll-neck blue sweater this morning. It was the first time Mark had seen him during daylight hours, but within the walls of this derelict filling station there seemed only dimness, after the brilliance of the sun outside.

The man handed over the supplies they had agreed without a word. Even in this dingy setting, he wore sunglasses with small, very black lenses, so that you could not see his eyes. His hands were surprisingly small and his movements very swift. Mark realized for the first time that his supplier could be nervous, too. This drugs business might be lucrative, but it was less straightforward and more dangerous than Mark had thought it would be.

There was more cannabis than Mark wanted, more than he had been able to shift in the school and on the previous night at the club. There were also small quantities, no more than a couple of grams, of the white and brown powders Mark knew were cocaine and heroin, and also some small squares of what looked like blotting paper, which puzzled him.

'LSD. Don't you even bloody recognize it?' said the man tersely. 'You don't need to pay now. But I'll want the money next time.'

'Sale or return?' said Mark. He tried to laugh and couldn't manage it.

'You'll shift them and deliver the money for future supplies at our next meeting. That's the way my system works, son.'

They were almost the only words they exchanged. The man left first, easing his BMW from behind the ruined building with scarcely a sound, then roaring away swiftly into the distance.

Mark Lindsay left two minutes later, pedalling his bicycle in the opposite direction, back towards the centre of the town and his home. He tried to ride swiftly, but the tiny packages in the pockets of his anorak seemed to weigh him down.

Martin Sheene had been expecting the call for days, but it was still a shock when it came.

He had given his statement to the detective constable at the school, waiting his turn on the list with the other teachers. He'd said no more than he had to say, been non-committal, even bored, as he sought to emphasize that this was no more than a fulfilment of police routine.

The voice on the phone was curiously unthreatening. It had

116

a thick local accent, Herefordshire or Gloucestershire. Not being a native of the area, Martin couldn't be sure which. It said, 'We need to ask you a few questions about the death of your headmaster, Mr Sheene.'

'You spoke to me at Greenwood School. Earlier in the week.'

'You made a statement to one of our officers, yes. This is a follow-up interview.'

'I can't think why you would need that. Is this happening to all the teachers who—'

'We're within a couple of hundred yards of you now. We'll be there within two minutes.'

They hadn't asked whether it would be convenient. He said desperately, 'Wouldn't this be better at the school? I could be there in half an hour. It would really suit me better to—'

'We'll be with you almost immediately, sir. We'll provide evidence of identity, if you require it.'

There wasn't time to ditch anything. Martin snatched up a couple of videos and put them away in the rather shabby cupboard beside his bookshelves. Then the doorbell rang and his inquisitors were in the house, almost before he realized that they were over the threshold: the Superintendent Lambert who had addressed them at Greenwood on Wednesday evening and his sidekick, the detective sergeant with the weather-beaten face who had just spoken to him on the phone.

They looked around the room, with its shabby furniture which he had bought with the house and never bothered to replace, its window which stubbornly refused to open, even though the sun was pouring through it now. They didn't miss much, these two: probably part of their training to assess the important things about a place at a glance. But there surely wasn't much visible here that could damage him? Martin had to resist the sensation that they knew all about him already, that they could see through wooden facings and into cupboards and drawers.

J.M. Gregson

Only when they had taken in his surroundings did they turn their attention to Martin. It was the sergeant, Hook, who said to him, 'I think you'd better sit down, Mr Sheene.' Fancy telling him what to do in his own house. He should have challenged such discourtesy. Instead he sat down meekly on an upright chair beside the table, his arm falling clumsily across its surface as he did so.

Hook flicked open a notebook as he sat down in Martin's favourite armchair. 'We'll just check a few facts first. You are Martin Algernon Sheene?'

That silly second name thrown in his face at the outset: he half-expected them to sneer at it, as boys had done long ago in the playground. 'Yes. My mum called me Algy, you see, when I was young. I changed to Martin as soon as I got away from home.'

'You went to university.'

'Yes, and then I did a Postgraduate Certificate in Education, so that I could teach.'

'And you're now thirty-two.'

'Yes. I've been teaching for ten years. Ever since I got my qualification. Geography principally, and a little basic science for the juniors.' He didn't want to volunteer information, but he didn't seem able to stop his tongue running.

'You're a single man. And you've never been married.'

'No.' He ran a hand through his lank hair, forced a smile. 'The right girl hasn't come along, yet!' Might as well assert his heterosexual credentials. They didn't like gays, the police.

'You've had a variety of posts.'

'Yes.' He tried again to keep silent, but when they didn't help him out, he said with a nervous giggle, 'One has a career to build, you know. One has to move around, gather experience.'

'I see. Your application for the post at Greenwood indicates that you've been in five posts in ten years, including your present one.'

118

They'd been into the staff files at the school! It set his mind racing, that thought. He made himself ask the question he did not want to voice. 'Been checking everyone's background, have you?'

Hook looked at his superintendent, who said lightly, 'Not everyone's, Mr Sheene. There hasn't really been time for that, as yet. We've only called for the ones which seemed of particular interest.'

This Lambert fellow seemed to be leading him towards a particular query, and Martin, as his mother had always claimed when he was in trouble, was easily led. He said, 'And why would my file be of particular interest to you?'

Lambert ignored the query. 'Would you say that five posts in ten years is usual, Mr Sheene?'

'Well, you have to gather experience, as I said.'

'You're well-qualified, Mr Sheene. You have a good degree from a good university.'

Martin forced a small smile. 'I like to think so.' They'd really been studying his background, by the sound of it.

'But you're still on the basic teaching scale at Greenwood. No special allowances. Not a head of department.'

'Some of us are more concerned with job satisfaction than with advancement in the profession.'

'I see. That hardly tallies with what you said about moving to advance your career, does it?'

The man's quiet manner belied his words: he was like a dog with a bone. And Martin knew now that he wasn't going to give up the bone. 'I think that's my business, isn't it?'

For the second time in two minutes, Lambert ignored his question and pressed on. 'Were you asked to leave any of your previous teaching posts, rather than choosing to move on of your own accord, Mr Sheene?'

It was inexorable. But Martin couldn't think what to do, other than struggle on like a fish floundering helplessly in a net at the water's edge. 'I want to do all I can to help you, of course I do, but this really is an unwarrantable intrusion into my private life, you know. I don't see why—'

'Are you refusing to answer?'

'Well, not exactly, but—'

'Perhaps it would be useful for you to know that I spoke to two of your former head teachers on the phone last night.'

The fish was on the bank now, flapping its last, helpless movements, fighting hopelessly for life. 'Nothing was ever proved. I moved on of my own accord.'

'Whilst you were still able to move, I presume. If anything had been proved against you, you would have gone on official blacklists, been unable to work again with children.'

Martin stared sullenly down at his forearm, still lying awkwardly on the table. 'Nothing was ever proved. I could sue anyone who says otherwise.'

'Which is why no one could put down anything against you in writing. Which is what allowed you to get the post at Greenwood Comprehensive.'

Martin dared not look up. His limbs desperately wanted to move, to leap into any form of action, but he held them stiff and rigid, as if rapid movement of his arms or legs would itself be a confession. He said, 'They were glad to get someone of my qualifications and experience to take a job on the basic scales. And I'm not a bad teacher; the children mostly like me. You ask—'

'That unfortunately is not the point at issue this morning, is it, Mr Sheene?'

'Isn't it? Well you'd better tell me what the point is, because frankly I don't see why I should take any—'

'The point at issue is how Peter Logan died. I think you should know that he made a phone call three days before he was killed, Mr Sheene. To the National Paedophile Unit at New Scotland Yard.'

Lambert waited for him to deny that he was the man concerned. But Martin Sheene was past that point. He said in scarcely more than a whisper, 'I haven't hurt any of the children at Greenwood Comprehensive. I wouldn't do that.'

'So you admit that you were the subject of Mr Logan's phone call?'

Dimly and too late, he realized that he had been tricked into an admission. 'I thought you just said that Logan had phoned this Paedophile Unit about me.'

'No. All I said was that he had phoned the National Paedophile Unit. He said he was concerned about a member of his teaching staff. He wished to discuss the matter in confidence with someone from the Unit.'

'So he didn't mention me.'

'No. Are you now denying that you were the member of staff concerned?'

It was familiar ground to Martin. He had been over it before, in other schools. He had always managed to get out before it got really nasty. They had to have solid evidence against you to take you to court, because the law was as tricky as a snake. Most people were happy to avoid the embarrassment of having employed you, if you moved out of their area, and his legal friends in the group had always advised him when to go.

But this was different. He had never got as far as being questioned by policemen before, let alone this quiet Torquemada of a superintendent. He was suddenly tired of running, weary of the whole pretence of being something he was not. He said exhaustedly, 'No. There doesn't seem any point in denying anything now, does there? Peter Logan found that I had taken children into the junior science laboratory with me during the lunch hour. He must have been ringing because of that.'

There was a long pause. They made a strange trio, the two experienced CID men sitting in easy chairs and the hopeless figure with the slumped shoulders at the table. Eventually Martin Sheene said, 'I haven't damaged any children. I – I'm fond of them, that's all. Perhaps too fond.' When there was no reaction to this, he slowly lifted his head to look at them. 'What happens now?'

Lambert nodded to Hook, who said quietly, 'Other people will have to take this matter up with you, in due course. I think you will be suspended on full pay, pending further inquiries into your conduct, but that of course will not be our decision. Superintendent Lambert and I are concerned solely with finding out who killed Peter Logan.'

'But you surely can't think I did that?' He said it limply, when there should have been outrage at the suggestion; he should have been on his feet in anger. But he could raise no energy for that. The time for simulating indignation was past.

Hook said, 'You must surely see that the situation you have now admitted gives you a strong motive to remove Mr Logan. He suspected he had a paedophile in his school, but he had not named you to anyone. Your whole career was at stake, your whole lifestyle. It's a strong motive for murder, Mr Sheene. Stronger than any other motive we have so far discovered, in fact.'

'I didn't kill him.' The words had the ring of a hopeless ritual.

Lambert took up the questioning again. 'Where were you on Monday night, Mr Sheene?'

'Here. On my own. I watched a little television, if I remember right.' He'd watched some of his videos acquired from the group, not the television; for a horrid moment, he expected them to ask him to give a rundown of the television programmes on Monday night.

Instead, Lambert said, 'I think we've established that you are a paedophile, Mr Sheene. Other people, more specialist officers in that field, will wish to discuss the details with you. What I have to ask you is whether you are a member of a paedophile ring.'

'Ring?'

Lambert sighed. He had never raised his voice above normal throughout their exchanges, yet Martin was inordinately afraid of him and what he might say next. 'Please don't try to be evasive at this stage, Mr Sheene. You must be well aware that people with your sexual preferences tend to get together in groups. I'm asking you whether you are a member of such a group.'

'No. I wouldn't – I've never wanted to be a member of a group like that.'

He was suddenly scared, and with fear he was reanimated, when a moment earlier he had thought himself too exhausted to resist. They mustn't find out about the ring and the people who were in it. If he split on them, there was no knowing what might happen to him. He said again, as if he could make it true by earnest repetition, 'There is no group. I'm not a member of any ring.'

Lambert studied him for a long moment, then stood up abruptly. He seemed to Martin even taller than when he had come into the room. 'Don't move out of the area, Mr Sheene. Not without letting us know at Oldford CID. Someone will be in touch with you over the weekend about the situation at the school.'

Martin watched them go, standing at the front window of his house for minutes after their car had turned the corner and disappeared. Then he went back into his house and began to fling video cassettes into plastic dustbin bags with a furious energy. With garden rubbish hastily crammed into the top sections to disguise the contents, they were consigned to the council dump within half an hour. Amidst the frenetic activity of an autumn Saturday at the site, his modest contribution was scarcely even noticed. The pathetic evidence of his involvement with the group disappeared before his gratified eyes.

In the Saturday quiet of Oldford CID, only the skeleton of the murder team was working. Superintendent John Lambert was arranging for a twenty-four hour surveillance to be kept on the comings and goings of Martin Sheene.

Fifteen

D aniel Price found that Saturday afternoon was a useful time to conduct the less official side of his business.

There was no one in the offices of Price Computer Supplies at this time. If the proprietor was seen in there on a Saturday, that only made him a more conscientious employer, working diligently to preserve the prosperity of his employees as well as himself. If he was prosperous, as he obviously was, then he obviously worked very hard for it and deserved his affluence. A model employer.

The succession of diverse humanity who visited him on this Saturday might have other views on his conduct as an employer, but they were in no position to voice them. The illegal drugs industry has no trade unions.

Two men, then a woman, each of them in charge of selling in different parts of Price's small but developing empire. They were doing well, these three, expanding their sales, pushing the Class A drugs which provided the greatest danger to the users but the highest profits for the suppliers. Daniel gave them appropriate encouragement, discussed with them their ideas for developing their markets still further. This was very much like his computer business, really, he thought, except that the profits were much bigger and you had to be much more careful.

His fourth and last visitor was another male, the one Mark Lindsay now thought of as 'the man in black'.

This man tried to anticipate the rebuke he felt was coming from Daniel Price. 'Business is a bit slack at the moment. It will probably pick up as we move into the winter.'

Daniel gave him his most patronizing smile. He was dispensable, this man. He already had someone else in mind for what he called 'the school run' if the man in black didn't pull his socks up. 'On the contrary, the other people I have seen today have talked to me of expanding sales. I'm very pleased with them.'

'I need to be a bit cautious with my school pushers, though. The police have been swarming around the place in the last few days because of this murder.'

He had a point there. But it wasn't Daniel's policy to allow sales staff to make points, in either of his businesses. He treated any acknowledgement of the difficulties as a sign of weakness; if you didn't admit the difficulties were there, good salesmen usually went ahead and solved the problems for themselves. 'The people in the school aren't Drugs Squad. They're not investigating our little business.'

'No. I'm trying to convey that message myself. But the pushers I have around the school and the club are only youngsters. They're bound to be scared, when they see the plods around.'

A more balanced employer than Daniel Price would have accepted the point, would have agreed that inexperienced dealers should lie low for a little while, until they got the feel of the ground and their users came back to them. But Daniel was greedy; he had so far known only success, and success is a demanding mistress.

He said, 'You've got a good market, in the comprehensive school and Shakers. An expanding market: the number of kids between fourteen and eighteen who are experimenting with drugs is going up by ten per cent each year. It's up to you to take advantage of that demand. The patch you've been fortunate enough to collect gives you the best chance of all of developing a market rapidly.'

He was almost convincing himself as he spoke. He had made up that percentage increase among teenagers, but the man in front of him was in no position to argue. The man in black said weakly, 'Perhaps the kids I've got working for me aren't quite up to it.'

'And whose fault would that be? I gave you a free hand in recruiting your staff.' Price couldn't possibly have done anything else: he knew nothing about the situation on the ground. But the man wouldn't dare point that out, probably wouldn't even dare to think it.

Like most bullies, Daniel Price got worse when there was no resistance. He said, 'You said there were rumours that the headmaster was on to something, that he had his suspicions about your pushers. Well, he's no longer on the scene, is he? I should have thought you'd be making hay while the sun shines.'

Mark Lindsay would have been amazed to see the man who frightened him so cowed. The man in black virtually apologized for his lack of expansion, then promised he would do better in the future. Daniel sent him on his way with a final sharp bollocking: that would keep the bugger on his toes.

As Daniel Price watched the car drive away, he smiled with satisfaction at the gee-up he had given to this last of his appointments for the day. He had not the slightest notion that he had just made a serious mistake.

Jane Logan opened the front door to them before they could knock. She said accusingly, 'Catriona's playing hockey for the school, so I'm on my own. That's just as well. It would have upset her to know you were coming here again, for the third time in four days.'

Lambert said, 'I'm sorry about that. I can understand her feelings. Perhaps a third visit wouldn't have been necessary, if you'd been completely honest with us during the first two.'

She didn't react to this, offering them nothing until she had them seated in the chairs she had planned for them in the comfortable sitting room. The chairs afforded them a splendid view over a garden whose autumn colours were especially vivid in the early October twilight. Though both men were looking not at the garden but at her. She said, 'If I told anything but the truth, it was quite unwitting. You might try allowing for the fact that I am in an emotional turmoil after the sudden and violent death of my husband.'

Nice try, Mrs Logan, thought Bert Hook as he flicked his notebook to a blank page. But you were perfectly composed last time we were here, at pains to tell us that the marriage was over and you weren't as grief-stricken as a widow might normally be. He looked expectantly at John Lambert, who was watching Jane Logan with a mordant smile.

The Superintendent took his time, waiting to see if his quarry might dig herself more deeply into the hole. Then he said quietly, 'Where were you on the night when your husband was killed, Mrs Logan?'

'On Monday night? I told you. I went to the gym for a bit of a workout. I must have been home by nine or nine thirty. When Peter hadn't come in at ten thirty, I went to bed. You've had all this from me before.'

'We have indeed. I just thought you might like to put the record straight. To tell us where you *really* were in those crucial hours when your husband was being brutally murdered.'

The hazel eyes on each side of the strong nose looked at them steadily. She must have known that she had been found out, but her face gave no indication of it. She said, 'I just told you, I went to the gym. This is beginning to seem like harassment.'

'Would it prompt a re-think if I told you that the gym you mentioned has no record of your visiting them on Monday night?'

She folded her arms, gave them a small smile to show that they had not shaken her. 'It's a busy place. Probably they didn't notice me. I mostly just ride one of the exercise bikes, and get on with it very quietly.'

Lambert shook his head. 'If you used the gym frequently, you'd be well aware that they book you in and monitor the equipment you're using. Their records show that you paid your subscription in March, but haven't used the place once since that initial visit.'

For a moment, it looked as if she would persist in her hopeless denials. She flushed, whether in embarrassment at being revealed as a liar or in anger at their challenge it was impossible to say.

When she spoke, she seemed to be forcing out the words. 'I'm sorry I tried to deceive you. I don't usually go in for lying. I can only say that I had my reasons.'

'Which you had better outline to us now.'

She shook her head. 'I can't do that.'

'On the contrary, you can and must. You of all people should not need to be reminded that this is a murder inquiry. There is no room for lies, and least of all for lies from the victim's widow.'

She was dressed formally, in a green suit which set off her dark-blonde hair: Hook wondered if she had put this on specially to meet them, though he had given her no more than ten minutes notice of their arrival when he phoned. Her only gesture towards mourning was a black chiffon scarf at her throat, to which her hand now rose. She looked a little older today, but no less attractive. Her appearance was dignified, which was ironic in view of the indignity she had just suffered in being unmasked as a liar.

She didn't hurry her reply, assessing her options, then apparently deciding she could do little other than tell them the truth. Or was this more acting? Was she really deciding to release to them her own limited version of the truth, still holding back things she thought she could safely conceal? Hook, studying her now as carefully as Lambert, could not be sure as she said, 'All right. I was with someone that night. As you may have guessed by now.'

'Who was that?'

'I'm not at liberty to say. I don't want that person dragged into this.'

'I'm afraid you do not have that choice, Mrs Logan. All I can say is that we will be as discreet as we can with the information, if it proves to have no bearing on this case.'

'I can assure you that it does not.'

'I'm afraid your assurances are not enough. Especially as you have so far decided to conceal the information. You must see that when you lie to us, we are likely to be intensely interested in whatever it is you have lied about. That is not personal; it applies to anyone involved in a serious crime investigation.'

She smiled acerbically. 'I should have thought a certain degree of sympathy would be accorded to the newly bereaved.'

Lambert gave her an answering smile: they were two people who understood each other, these two, thought Bert Hook. But that meant that Jane Logan wouldn't get away with anything. The Superintendent said, 'You must see that you have forfeited any sympathy by lying to us. Even now, you did not volunteer the truth but denied it for as long as you could. You could be accused of obstructing the police during a murder investigation. You had much better tell us the truth now – the complete truth.'

She nodded. 'I was with a man. You probably guessed that.'

'We try not to make guesses. We prefer that people answer our questions accurately.'

'My children do not know about this. I should prefer that things remained like that, for the present.'

'No guarantees, I'm afraid, beyond the assurance I've already given to you. You've held us up for quite long enough, Mrs Logan. Who was the man you were with on Monday night?'

She looked for a moment as if she would still resist. Then she said tersely, 'It was Steve Fenton. He – he used to be—'

'Used to be Chairman of the Governors at your husband's

school, yes. We spoke to Mr Fenton this morning. But I expect you know all about that meeting. I'm sure you've been comparing notes from the start about what we were doing.'

She didn't deny it. 'We have our reasons for the secrecy. Steve has just gone through a very messy divorce case: his wife is a vindictive woman and would take any opportunity to cut down his access to his children.'

'You told us in our last interview that your marriage was not a happy one. Did your husband know about your association with Mr Fenton?'

'No. I told you yesterday that Peter had bedded a succession of women. Perhaps he wouldn't have got too excited about Steve and me. No doubt he would have called it a quick fuck on the side.' She threw all the bitterness of a failed marriage into the last ugly phrase.

Lambert said quietly, 'And is that what it was?'

'No. It was the first and only time that I'd strayed from my marriage vows, though God knows I've had cause enough to. But it was a serious relationship. Steve and I will get married.'

'But you weren't prepared to say so publicly.'

'I've told you Steve's situation. And whatever I thought of Peter, I wasn't going to destroy his career. Headmasters are still rather like clergymen: they aren't supposed to get divorced.'

'You think it would have damaged your husband's career?'

'It would have damaged all of us, Mr Lambert. Peter had enjoyed a lot of publicity as he built up an outstanding school. You must know how media people work: the same ones who've built you up delight in knocking you down. You can imagine what the tabloids would have made of this. "Brilliant headmaster works long hours in school whilst his wife enjoys a quick leg-over with the chairman of his governors." And much more in that vein. I wouldn't wish that on my worst enemy. And Peter was far from that.'

'Would he have given you a divorce?'

'No. It would have damaged his career too much. We'd already discussed it, long before Steve was on the scene; I wanted us to split up once the children had reached eighteen, but Peter wouldn't have it.'

'So what would be happening to you and Mr Fenton now if your husband was still alive?'

'I don't know. Peter didn't even know about Steve and me – he was far too wrapped up in his own affairs, professional and private. I'd have wanted a divorce, Peter would have opposed it; he'd have thrown the children into the argument, said a quick shag didn't warrant a divorce, refused to accept that Steve and I were anything more than that, and generally made things very messy.'

Lambert watched Hook making a note on his page. He had caught the anger in her obscenity and was waiting to see if she would go further. When she remained silent, he said, 'So you now say that you were with Mr Fenton on Monday evening. For how long?'

She did the right thing, appearing to think about her statement. She had in fact decided what she must say before they came. 'From about seven thirty to ten. I couldn't be precise about the times: I didn't think I was going to be asked about them by senior CID officers at the time.'

'And those officers didn't expect to find the widow of a murder victim lying about her movements at the time of his death,' rejoined Lambert dryly. 'Is there anyone else who can vouch for the fact that you and Mr Fenton were together during those hours?'

'No. Would you expect there to be?' She let her smile emphasize how ridiculous the question was.

Lambert did not return the smile. He kept his scrutiny steadily upon the intelligent face opposite him as he said evenly, 'I wouldn't expect that, no. But it would be useful from your own point of view if someone could confirm this, since you and Mr Fenton have previously steadily denied that it was so.'

She was nettled a little, despite her resolution to remain calm. 'It was surely understandable that Steve and I should wish to keep things quiet. We both have children, for a start. Steve's are still adjusting to a divorce; he's trying to maintain contact with his two. Mine have just lost their father in the most distressing circumstances. We should like to tell them about our relationship in our own time, not let them hear some sensationalized account of it from the tabloids.'

Lambert nodded tersely. 'So you decided to lie in a murder investigation. To obstruct the course of the law. Mrs Logan, it must surely be apparent to you that you have just been outlining a perfect motive for murder. For you; for Mr Fenton; for both of you together.'

She looked for a moment as if she would shout defiance at him. But in the end she took her cue from his coolness, meeting the stare of the grey eyes with a defiant calm of her own. 'All right, I understand that. I cannot expect you to have the same perspective on events as I have. All I can do is to assure you that I didn't kill Peter, and neither did Steve.'

'Then I suggest you give some thought to who might have done. Despite what you have said about your marriage, you must have known the people who were around your husband better than anyone. Think about it, then give us your thoughts in confidence – more frankly than you have done previously.'

They stood up. Jane Logan could scarcely believe that in the end they were going very swiftly. Then Lambert paused in the doorway. He had daughters of his own, older than this woman's, with children of their own now. But he remembered the crises of their adolescence. He said, 'Mrs Logan, we gathered when we interviewed the manageress at the gym that her daughter is a friend of your daughter. I suspect from what she said that Catriona knows that you have not been visiting the gym when you told her you were going there. I just thought you might like to be made aware of that.'

Jane let them go with no more than a nod of thanks for the warning about her daughter.

She told herself that she had always known it would come to this, in the end. She should have listened to Steve from the start. He had always said that they should tell the police about their affair, acknowledge that they had a motive for murder, and then defy the police to find the evidence to arrest them.

She dialled his number hastily now. 'They know!' she said. It was the only phrase she could get out.

Sixteen

M ark Lindsay didn't want to face the wrath of the man in black again. He decided he must push the drugs harder. And more often. He would make a start right away, on this Saturday night.

But life immediately provided a diversion. Life, Mark was beginning to learn, was like that. The girl he had been forced to snub on the previous night turned up at Shakers ten minutes after his early arrival and beamed at him. She had not, after all, been irreparably insulted. She seemed, on the contrary, more friendly than ever. Perhaps she had thought he was playing hard to get.

Mark Lindsay was still inexperienced enough to speculate about the female psyche.

Her name was Ellie Peters. She was blonde, with small, pretty features, a smile which lit up her unlined face, and curves beneath her dress that had Mark suppressing a groan of desire. All these delights in one small, exquisitely female person, and she was speaking to him.

'Didn't think you'd be here again tonight,' she said. 'You must be a rich man to come to this place twice in a weekend.' It was all she could think of to say. To Mark it sounded like the epitome of wit, the kind of thing those French women had set up salons to hear in centuries past.

He said, 'Oh, I have my moments, you know. And I'm glad I made the effort, now that I see you here again.' It was almost a witty riposte; he was very nearly at ease, making conversation with this goddess.

It was easier than he had thought possible. In a few minutes they were dancing, on a floor which was still uncrowded because it was early in the evening. And when the dance was over she said she had enjoyed it. Mark could scarcely reply: he was still trying to memorize every movement of her sinuous body, ready for instant recall in his later erotic fantasies.

He had always felt at a disadvantage when his fellows, newly arrived in the sixth form with him, enlarged upon their sexual conquests. He decided now that on Monday he would merely smile quietly and enigmatically when the moment came, keeping his own counsel. He would not demean Ellie by boasting about her soft flesh and what he had achieved with it. He was such a gentleman at heart, as his mother had always said.

He had never been alone with anyone so enchanting before, never made conversation with a really pretty girl like this for so long. Mark, who played second violin in the school orchestra, thought that this must be what it was like to be a soloist. You had to concentrate for every second, were exposed on all the high notes. It was almost a relief when Ellie Peters said she was going to the ladies' cloakroom.

It was whilst she was away that he saw the man in black at the other end of the room. Standing there watching him. Like a ghost. Come here to whet his almost blunted purpose. That was *Hamlet*, which Mark had just started to study for A level and didn't understand at all. Well, he understood that bit well enough now, at any rate.

He shot off to the gents, stationed himself near the door. As luck would have it, two of his customers from school came in as soon as he had taken up his post. They renewed their order for grass, but turned down his suggestion of coke or horse. They couldn't afford it, full stop. He agreed that the exchange for the cannabis would take place in school on Tuesday morning, when they all had a free period.

There was the faint, sweet smell of cannabis from one of the cubicles. Mark waited until the man came out and went across to the washbasins for a desultory rinse of his hands. 'Quiet tonight,' said Mark.

The man agreed that it was. They watched each other warily in the big mirror over the basins as he dried his hands, as if to look directly at each other would imply more commitment than either wanted to admit to at this stage.

Mark recognized him. Although he did not know his name, he had seen him here before. The youth was perhaps two years older than Mark, but he hadn't attended Greenwood School; perhaps he had been a public schoolboy at the Cheltenham School for Boys. In which case he would have plenty of money. And he was already a user of pot. Mark put him down as a promising prospect. He was desperate to say something before the prosperous young man should turn and leave him. He forced a smile and said, 'It's so quiet here tonight that you need something to liven it up, don't you think?'

The older boy smiled briefly, and Mark realized with a shaft of surprise that he was as nervous as he was. The youth suddenly pulled out a comb from his back pocket and slicked it unnecessarily through his neatly parted brown hair. He addressed Mark's image in the mirror: 'You offering to provide something?'

'Spliffs,' said Mark promptly. Then, when his elder didn't react, he said hurriedly, 'There's other stuff available as well if you want it. Good-quality stuff. Coke and horse and – and LSD if you want it.' It had all tumbled out too hurriedly, making him into too eager a seller, but you never knew when you were going to be interrupted, he told himself.

The well-dressed youth had sensed his nervousness now. He smiled, took his time, prepared himself to patronize this eager young seller. 'Grass will do nicely, for the present, thank you. What's your price?'

'Twenty quid for thirty spliffs,' said Mark. 'And it's good quality, as I said. You won't—'

'I can get them cheaper in the precinct,' said the older man. 'You'll have to do better than that to beat my regular supplier.' There was no such being, but he divined correctly that Mark was anxious to make a sale, too anxious to haggle for long about the price.

They settled on fifteen quid for the thirty spliffs, which left Mark a very slender margin of profit. But he told himself he had made a new customer, that he was developing new markets, as he had been bidden by the man in black. He said hopefully, 'And you'll give serious consideration to whether you'd like some of the harder stuff. I can even do Rohypnol, you know.'

'Can you, indeed? In that case, I shall give the matter "serious consideration" as you suggest.' The youth inspected his reflection again, then turned away from the mirror and smiled mockingly down into the eager young face. 'But that's all for today, thank you.'

'I'm here every week. Tell your friends I can supply good stuff at competitive rates, won't you?' But Mark found that he was reciting his sales spiel to a door which was shutting slowly in his face on its automatic spring.

At least it was a sale. And he had acquired a new customer, a man who might bring other clients in his wake, in due course. He had sold at too low a price, but he would regard it as a loss leader, designed to expand his markets and bring the punters in. He liked that word 'punters'. He would try to think of his future customers as punters from now on: the very sound of the word would make him feel superior to them.

Mark went back and talked to Ellie, had another dance, bought her a Coke with lordly generosity. The club was filling up to its full Saturday night capacity now. In between the bouts of noisy music, people greeted each other and moved across the floor to form tight little groups among the rising tide of enjoyment. Mark was part of one of them. With Ellie by his side among eight of his peers from the sixth form, the world was a happy place. He felt more than adequate now to cope with the world, empowered by his secret status as a dealer.

He saw the man in black once more at the other end of the room, his face appearing and disappearing behind the mass of gyrating bodies. Mark watched anxiously for another sighting of his supplier, but there was none, and after another half hour he was convinced that he was gone. The thought lifted his spirits. Even when Ellie was carried off to dance with one of his friends, she kept smiling reassuringly at him as she tapped her feet and writhed her body to the rhythm, emphasizing to him that she was his girl now, that he could safely let her out of his keeping for a few minutes.

He went off to the main toilets at the other end of the big room. He arrived there as the dance finished and the crowds flocked in, exchanging noisy views on girls, the afternoon's football results, and life in general. Mark went and sat in one of the cubicles, waiting for the insistent thump of the music to begin again on the other side of the wall, listening to the crowd thinning in the tiled room outside the door with its scratched obscenities.

He had judged it right. Only a couple of youths who were even younger than he was were in the toilets now, and they left without a curious glance at Mark Lindsay, who stood with his back to them, watching them surreptitiously in the mirror.

A moment later, a man came into the cloakroom, looked briefly around it, then pulled a spliff from his shirt pocket, lit it, and puffed out a long, appreciative breath. Only then did he pay any attention to Mark, as if he was noticing him for the first time. 'Good stuff, this. The world seems a better place, when you look at it through a haze of pot smoke!'

Mark smiled back at him. 'You've got it right there, mate!' This man was older than his previous customer, and much less smooth. He had tight blue jeans and a Next shirt which had seen better times. He hadn't shaved for a couple of days at least, and the stubble was black and thick upon his chin and the neck beneath, emphasizing the brightness of the gold ring in his ear. He was perhaps six or seven years older than Mark, but friendly enough, and probably with money: despite his clothing, he carried the air of confidence that usually went with money.

He looked the kind who might be in the market for the heavier stuff, for the Class A drugs that Mark knew he had to push to make himself big money. And he seemed in no hurry to leave. Mark determined to pitch his spiel more carefully to these promising ears.

He said as casually as he could, 'Happy with your supplier, are you?'

'I might be. Might not. You in the market?'

Mark smiled. 'Supply you with as much of that stuff as you want, mate. Do you a good price, as well.'

The man pursed his lips, scratched his chin a little to play for time, his nails rasping against the black stubble. But Mark could see he was interested. The thin face looked at the open doors of the cubicles, reassuring itself that there were no hidden witnesses to this. 'I'm ready to buy, but I can get pot any time I want. Do any of the harder stuff, do you?'

It was almost too good to be true. Mark forced himself to pause for a moment, looking round the room cautiously as the man beside him had done, though he was well aware that they were alone. 'I can do the lot, mate. Coke, horse, LSD, Ecstasy.' He grew expansive, leaned a little nearer to his man, fancied he smelt the sweat upon him, felt a further lift from that. 'You name it, mate, and we can do it. Good stuff at good prices.'

The man's eyes flashed his excitement. They glittered blue in the swarthy face. 'How much is the horse?'

'Hundred and ten pounds a gram. Good stuff mind, not rubbish! Five grams for five hundred pounds.'

He'd left himself a few pounds to barter with, so that the man could feel he'd beaten him down, got himself a bargain. But the chin nodded acceptance as the blue eyes narrowed craftily. 'You do Rohypnol?'

Mark was almost enjoying it now. Perhaps he was a natural salesman after all. Maybe in a few years he'd be doing well for himself in something more legitimate – selling Jaguar cars or expensive furniture perhaps. But he must concentrate on closing a deal here. He let his lips frame a soundless whistle at the mention of the date-rape drug. 'We can do it, mate, but it will cost. Doesn't come cheap, Rohypnol – but then, look what it can do for you with the girls!'

Mark's attempt at a conspiratorial leer was not all that successful, but he was pleased to see his companion nodding at the thought. Mark moved a little nearer to the ear with the gold ring, preparing to clinch a deal on the hard drugs, where the big profits were.

But it was his ear into which the words were breathed. There was an agonizing flash of white pain through his head as his arm was twisted high into his back. Then the words gushed in a rapid stream into his ear: 'I arrest you on suspicion of attempting to deal in Class A drugs. You do not have to say anything, but it may harm your defence if you do not mention when questioned something which you later rely on for your defence in court. Anything you do say will be recorded and may be given in evidence.'

Mark Lindsay scarcely heard the last of the words. He was conscious only of the agony in his arm, of the searing pain which seemed to go from his arm through his shoulder blades and up into his head. He gasped, 'You're breaking my arm, mate!'

The voice was harsh in his ear now; he felt the bristles like wire against his neck. 'On the contrary, there are another two inches to go to break it. We'll move out of here quietly now. Any attempt to get away and I will break this arm, for sure. You're well and truly nicked. Mate!'

The man moved him through the main room of the club almost at a trot, with his left arm still held against his back in a grip of steel. Just before he went out into the cold dark of the night, Mark caught a glimpse of Ellie Peters' pretty, astonished face.

He tried to smile reassuringly at her, but failed totally.

Seventeen

S unday morning is normally a quiet time in police stations. The Saturday night drunks have mostly been sent on their way, charged or uncharged, and apart from the odd weekend 'domestic', the station sergeant does not expect to be much troubled.

It is very rare indeed for an attractive young woman to present herself on a Sunday morning and say she has valuable information to divulge. The desk sergeant pushed aside his mug of tea and his *Sunday Sport* and prepared to give this member of the public a model display of police diligence. He was quite disappointed when he found that she was a candidate for CID attention. He took her through reluctantly to where Detective Inspector Rushton sat at his computer.

A less conscientious officer than DI Rushton might not have been there at all at 9.20 a.m. on a Sunday. But Chris had not found himself another partner since his divorce, and the neat but sterile little flat he was now forced to inhabit was a lonely place, though he did not care to admit that to his fellow officers. Loneliness tended to make a man conscientious.

She was small and very pretty, in a healthy, buxom sort of way. She was a natural blonde, with shoulder-length golden hair and a fresh, unlined complexion. She had never been in a police station before. When the magic word 'murder' ushered her straight through into CID and set her in front of a hastily rising DI Rushton, she was a little disconcerted by the place.

She was bubbly and cheerful by nature, and she knew

enough of life by now to understand that these were attractive qualities to the opposite sex, so she did not normally curb them. But early on Sunday morning in a police station, she found herself a little subdued.

To Chris Rushton her confusion was rather fetching. He explained to her about how murder rooms were set up, about the machinery of a murder investigation, about forensic laboratories, about how anything which might eventually prove to be an exhibit in court had to be carefully labelled and enclosed in polythene.

If there had been other people around, Chris would have been brisk and efficient, even impatient with his visitor. But now he took his time, trying to give the girl confidence as that annoyingly successful Bert Hook might have done. He found it an unexpectedly enjoyable process.

Statistically – and no one knew his statistics better than DI Rushton – there was every chance that this enchanting Sunday morning presence would be nothing more than a time-waster: most people who volunteered information in a murder investigation were no more than that. But this might just be the exception, and it came packaged in a wholly diverting form.

The girl took the initiative herself in the end. 'You must wonder why I've come here. Well, I've had a sleepless night again. I decided I couldn't keep quiet about this any longer.'

'That's usually much the best course. If it proves to have nothing to do with the victim's death, we shall be discreet.' Chris smiled encouragement to mitigate the formality of phrases he had used many times before. 'May I have your name and address, please?'

'Liza Allen. I work at the school where Peter Logan was the headmaster.'

'At Greenford Comprehensive? But all the teaching staff have given us statements. I don't recall—'

'That's just it. I'm not teaching staff. I've been expecting someone to ask me for a statement but no one has been near me so far.'

'What do you do at the school?'

'I'm a lab assistant. In the science laboratories.'

Chris typed the information rapidly on to his computer screen. He said in his most avuncular manner, 'Now, Liza, you must have something you think is going to be useful to us, or you wouldn't—'

'Peter was coming to see me, on the night he died. I live near the park where he was killed. Three streets away. Not more than three hundred yards from where . . .' She was suddenly in tears, and they came not just without warning but in floods, shaking her whole frame, shuddering the top of the blonde head as it fell forward, making Chris yearn to spring from his chair and put his arm tenderly round the trembling shoulders.

He did no such thing, of course. He said stiffly, 'What makes you think that, Miss Allen?'

She looked up at him as if he had accused her of murdering the man herself. 'I don't think it, I know it! He'd arranged it the day before, then he rang me at lunch time from Birmingham to confirm it.'

'You were lovers?'

'Yes. Of course we were!'

She spoke as if there could have been nothing more obvious. He resisted the urge to type this latest fact into his machine as she watched him. He kept his voice even as he said, 'It's taken you a long time to come forward.'

She nodded, was about to speak when she was wracked by another bout of sobbing. 'It – it was our secret. It was all I had left. And Peter has – had a family. I didn't want to cause pain for his wife and children, did I?'

Chris Rushton had to resist a sudden, surprising urge to take this silly girl by the shoulders and shake some sense into her. She was probably no more than six or seven years younger than he was. Why had she chosen to complicate her life with this ageing philanderer with his family baggage, when she could have had an eager young detective inspector with no ties? He said sternly, like a father-confessor, 'And how long had this liaison been going on?'

'Not long. A couple of weeks. We'd only – well, we hadn't been lovers for long at all.' Perhaps she saw the pity in his eyes, because she suddenly shouted, 'And I realize I wasn't the first. I'm not stupid, you know!'

He looked hastily around. He wasn't used to dealing with emotional young women, but fortunately there seemed to be no curious observers of their exchange. 'Of course you're not stupid, Liza. And you've done the right thing to make a clean breast of this.' He wished he hadn't used that particular metaphor as he watched her chest heaving impressively in front of him. 'What we need to ascertain now is whether you can tell us anything which might help us to find out who killed Mr Logan. I'm sure you're as anxious as we are that we should arrest the person responsible as soon as possible.'

She nodded, unable to speak, and he feared the tears would burst out again. Instead she said, the words coming all in a rush, 'It was that woman. I thought you'd have arrested her by now.'

Rushton was at a loss. He said woodenly, 'A woman at Greenwood School, you mean?'

'That damned teacher! Peter was in love with me, you see, and she knew it! She told me she wasn't going to let him get away with it. Those were her very words!'

DI Rushton knew now who she meant. He already had a file on this woman in his computer. But he wanted the accusation to come from those lips which seemed to him so red, so tender and so tremulous. So Chris said quietly, 'And who would this be, Liza?'

'Tamsin Phillips, of course.'

Steve Fenton was expecting the visit. He had been waiting for it since eight o'clock. By ten, he was quite nervous.

Lambert didn't make the conventional apology for disturbing him on a Sunday morning. Fenton had forfeited his rights to courtesy by withholding information on the previous day. Perhaps he realized that, for he seemed embarrassed as he led them into the tidy sitting room and offered them coffee.

To Bert Hook's delight, the offer was accepted. Fenton endured another five minutes of tense speculation in his kitchen before he set the tray down and handed round the cups. He was conscious of Hook flicking his notebook open ostentatiously as he munched his first bite of ginger nut. Finally Steve said, 'I'm sorry I wasn't completely honest with you at our previous meeting.'

Lambert did not smile. 'It would have been very much better if you had been.'

'Yes, I can see that now. I've never been involved in a murder investigation before. It rather throws one's judgement.'

'So it would appear. It also makes investigating officers treat your subsequent statements with an extra degree of suspicion.'

'I accept that. But you must see how we felt. The dead man's wife and her secret lover, wondering what to do about a husband who will not countenance a divorce. It's a classic B-movie motive for murder.'

'Which is made all the stronger when the people involved try to conceal their association after the murder. If you had set out to make us suspect the pair of you, you could hardly have gone about things better. Where were you on Monday night, Mr Fenton?'

'I was here. Exactly as I told you yesterday. From six thirty onwards. The only difference is that Jane Logan was with me for most of the evening.'

Hook looked up from his notebook and said tersely, 'Times, please.'

Even this stolid, easy-going sergeant was treating him like a criminal now, thought Steve. He made himself take a sip of the coffee he did not want before he said, 'From seven thirty until ten o'clock.'

Exactly the times Jane Logan had given them herself. But you would have expected that: they must have conferred on this, and they weren't going to contradict each other over anything so straightforward. Lambert as usual had never taken his eyes off his man. He said, 'So you are now giving each other an alibi for the time of the murder. Is there anyone else who could verify the fact that you were in this house for the whole of that time?'

'No. Would you expect there to be?'

'It would be helpful to you as well as to us if there were. All we are trying to do is to establish facts.'

'I'm sorry. We were together for two and a half hours. I should think we spent over half of that time in bed. You wouldn't really expect there to be any witnesses, however helpful one might be to us and to you.'

'No one phoned you during the evening? Even a telephone conversation would prove that you at least were here.'

Steve finished the biscuit he had bitten into earlier, finding it like cinders in his dry mouth. 'I hadn't thought of that. But no. No one phoned me on Monday night.' He managed a smile. 'I might have let the answerphone record a message if anyone had, since I was otherwise engaged in more pleasurable activities.'

Lambert looked him steadily in the face, wondering if Fenton was covering himself against the fact that they might find someone who had rung an empty house on Monday evening. He said abruptly, 'Why didn't you tell us yesterday that you had an expertise in firearms?'

Steve was shaken, as the Superintendent had intended that he should be. But he made himself speak deliberately. 'You didn't ask me about it. And I didn't see that it was relevant to your inquiry.'

'When a man has half his head blown away with a Smith and Wesson revolver?'

'Because of that very fact, Superintendent Lambert. No expertise is needed to place a revolver against a man's head and blow it away.'

It was a fair enough point, and Lambert acknowledged it with a thin smile. 'All the same, when a man is shot through the head, it seems odd not to mention that you have won prizes for shooting.'

'Modest prizes. At a local shooting club. Not at Bisley, Superintendent.'

'You own a revolver, I believe.'

Steve Fenton smiled. He was getting used to Lambert's sudden enquiries, had recognized that they were a tactic. 'I used to own one. Not any more. I gave up shooting and my membership of the rifle and small arms club when the regulations were tightened after that awful multiple shooting at Hungerford. I gave my pistol to the club: I haven't held a licence for years now.'

'I see. Have you had any further thoughts on who might have killed Peter Logan?'

Lambert had expected nothing, but Fenton furrowed his brow and said hesitantly, 'The school has a drugs problem, I believe. In that, it is no different from practically any large secondary school in the land. Peter Logan was aware of it, as he was aware of practically everything which went on in the place. I just wonder if he'd found out something which it was dangerous for him to know.'

Lambert studied him for a moment before he spoke, trying to work out if this was a genuine suggestion or an attempted diversion. 'It's possible, of course. It's a line of enquiry we're pursuing, along with several others. But if Mr Logan had found anything significant, he hadn't contacted the police in Cheltenham about it.'

'I see. Well, that wouldn't surprise me. He had a habit of hugging things to himself until he knew for certain, did Peter. And he was always very sensitive about anything which might damage the image of his school. He wouldn't have wanted to stir up a hornets' nest about drugs if he could possibly avoid it.'

'There's a possibility Logan's death could have a drugs connection, but no more than that. My own feeling is that someone less anonymous and nearer to him killed him.'

Lambert's exit was as abrupt as his questioning. He left on what sounded to Steve Fenton something very like a threat.

Eighteen

E ven detectives on a murder case must relax. The public does not like to accept it, but all sharpness, all sense of proportion, leaves them if they do not keep in touch with the more innocent world outside murder.

Lambert decided that Hook should continue his golfing education. On a bright, serene October afternoon, when there was a pleasant warmth in the sun, Bert, still a tyro in the game despite his nineteen handicap, was taken out to partner his chief at Ross-on-Wye Golf Club. He began by topping his drive horribly down the first.

'Shame to waste a lovely day like this on such a bloody silly game!' said Hook. He was still missing the cricket he had played for Herefordshire for twenty years, still not reconciled to the relentless advance of the years that was condemning the doughty fast bowler to the effete game of golf.

But he was determined about one thing. He would stem the flow of his chief's tuition at source. When he saw John Lambert advancing into the fringe of his vision to give him advice, he held up a lordly hand and delivered his prepared statement. 'I shall conduct my game without the benefit of your tutoring today, John,' he said. 'We are out here to relax and enjoy ourselves, and I find your guidance prevents me from doing either of those things.'

That's telling the old bugger, Bert thought, as he marched away to his ball. He put his second shot on to the green with a majestic six iron. Bert was surprised, but he had already learned enough about golf to behave as if this was no more

149

than his normal game and he had expected it. From the corner of his eye, he saw John Lambert looking stupefied – whether at the rejection of his advice or the splendour of his partner's stroke, it was impossible to say.

Bert Hook was soon distracted from such considerations by the eccentricities of the opposition. George Ollerenshaw was a tubby little man of fifty-eight who had not played any other game than golf to an acceptable standard. He attempted to make up for this omission by the seriousness he brought to the golf course in what we euphemistically call 'middle age' – there was mercifully little chance that George Ollerenshaw would live to be a hundred and sixteen.

He was that irritating phenomenon with which all seasoned golfers are familiar: the man who has an excuse for every bad shot. Bert Hook, still relatively inexperienced in the game, had not met anyone like this before. In Bert's view, you approached a dead ball in your own time and hit it when you were ready. In this decadent game, you could not get a ball screaming towards your crotch at ninety miles an hour or a ridiculous lbw decision. Anything you did was patently your own fault and there could be no excuses.

George Ollerenshaw had a million excuses.

For a start, he never got a good lie, even in the middle of the fairway, though the wretchedness was never remarked upon until after he had mishit the ball. The most wretched of topped shots, the most extravagant slice, the complete foozle, were all explained in turn as the work of the malevolent devil who set down George's ball in the wickedest places.

Men take their sport seriously. It is one thing which distinguishes them from lower forms of life. Bert Hook was a legend for his equanimity when confronted with the most foul-mouthed and blasphemous of criminals. But he was outraged by Ollerenshaw's refusal to confront sporting reality. When the corpulent one slashed the ball extravagantly out of bounds on the sixth and claimed for the fourth time in the round that he had been in a divot hole, Bert could stand it no longer.

'Golf,' he observed loudly to no one in particular but to the world at large, 'is a game in which the ball invariably lies badly and the player lies well.'

There was an embarrassed silence, whilst Bert strode forward, Ollerenshaw stared at him in outrage, and the other two men in the game looked hard at the blue sky above them.

'He's been studying for an Open University degree,' Lambert eventually said apologetically. 'I expect he's been reading too much.'

Ollerenshaw was quiet for a while. But his trouble was endemic, and the disease surfaced again within three holes. He was affected by the mewing of a buzzard half a mile away, by the scarcely audible laughter of golfers three holes ahead, by the low sun in his eyes, by the first of the autumn leaves drifting across his vision as he addressed his ball. Lambert gave Hook a series of increasingly desperate warning glares.

When George dispatched his ball irretrievably into the middle of the pond from the twelfth tee, it gave Bert Hook immense but initially secret satisfaction. The man could surely claim nothing in mitigation this time. He had chosen his own perfect lie, had set the ball up carefully upon his tee-peg. Rank bad shot, Your Honour. Plead guilty and ask for mitigation on the grounds of incompetence.

Ollerenshaw studied the widening circle of ripples on the still, dark water. He picked up his tee-peg with a huge sigh. Then he said, 'I should have stopped. The whiff of diesel from that tractor was quite overpowering.' He gestured with a wide sweep of his arm towards the farmer's fields on the left and the invisible and odourless machinery, then shook his head sadly and moved hopelessly towards his trolley.

Lambert commiserated hastily before Hook could express his outrage. '"The slings and arrows of outrageous fortune",' he called vaguely but sympathetically after the waddling back.

George turned a red and uncomprehending face.

'*Hamlet*,' explained Lambert, desperately avoiding Hook beside him.

Light dawned upon Ollerenshaw. 'The cigar advert,' he nodded.

Bert could be restrained no longer. 'No. The tragic Dane. Contemplating suicide at the time.' It seemed to Bert like an excellent suggestion for George.

The light dawned. 'Shakespeare. Never read it,' said George, as if that dismissed the matter for ever. Then, perhaps feeling a need to emphasize his erudition in the face of this humble plod, 'Tragedy, I think. He gets killed at the end.'

Hook nodded. 'Most people think death is a tragedy. But I can think of cases where it would be justifiable homicide.'

Lambert and Hook won handsomely. Lambert was wondering how to handle the after-match drinks when Rushton rang him with the news of Liza Allen's visit to the station. He seized eagerly upon the need to depart at once.

It seemed unlikely that George Ollerenshaw would ask them for a return match.

The man in black was nervous. He was pushing his team hard, because he was being pushed himself by Daniel Price.

But he wasn't happy. When you were breaking the law, you should proceed with caution, in his view. Grow the business slowly, but surely; make certain that each operative you put in place was working effectively before you went on to further expansion. There was a lot of money in this business, but there was danger as well: you should expect that when the profit was so huge. It paid you to be very, very careful.

Daniel Price didn't seem to appreciate that. He was trying to rake in the profits too quickly. Perhaps Price was himself being pushed by those above him. More likely he was simply greedy. But there was no one you could appeal to over his head. You simply didn't know who was next in line above him. The big boys, the barons who made their millions out of drugs, thrived on secrecy. No one knew anything about the chains of command above them, and most people only knew one person, their immediate superior and their contact with the supply chain.

The man in black felt very vulnerable.

He was doing things against his better judgement, which is always a danger sign. He knew that he should keep as low a profile as possible, be unseen but effective. You weren't selling the stuff yourself, so most of the time there was no need to be around. You only went to the clubs to recruit new staff or, very occasionally, to keep your existing staff up to the mark.

Yet on the night of Sunday, the fourth of October, he found himself going again to Shakers club in the town centre. He was like a mother hen, he thought, keeping his eye on his pushers, anxious to encourage, cajole, threaten them into increasing their sales. Bloody Daniel Price!

He was beginning to wish he had never recruited young Mark Lindsay. The lad wasn't reliable enough. He was naive. He was going to need constant supervision. But the man had needed someone to sell for him at Greenwood School: he had lost two pushers, a boy and a girl, who had moved out of the town when they left the sixth form. Young Lindsay had been both easily frightened and eager to make money. But that didn't make him a reliable pusher.

He'd have another look at Lindsay in action tonight. He might take the pressure off him a little, discourage him from taking silly risks. Or he might dispense with him altogether, whilst there was still time.

It was a clear night, but the moon wasn't yet up. The man in black found the blanket of darkness such a comfort that he almost turned away at the last moment. But that would have been silly, having come this far. He had to force

153

himself to leave the night and go into the brightness of the club.

It took him quarter of an hour to be certain that Mark Lindsay wasn't there. He circled the floor, where the noise level was already high and the temperature was rising in parallel with testosterone levels. He checked among the groups of noisy young men at the bar, then in both of the men's toilets.

Nothing wrong with that, he told himself. Perhaps the lad was merely keeping a low profile, doing what he now planned to advise him to do. Somehow it didn't seem likely. After all, it was only yesterday that he had been pressurizing Lindsay to sell more, putting the frighteners on him a bit. He regretted that now, and more so when the lad wasn't here.

His mind was full of young Lindsay when he went out again into the car park and the anonymity of the night. Perhaps he wasn't as vigilant as he would normally have been. Certainly he never saw the man, though he must have tracked him for sixty yards.

The man in black was leaning against the side of his car with his keys in his hand, wondering where he should go from here, when he felt the hand on his shoulder. A voice said quietly, 'Don't turn round. Raise your arms slowly and place them on the roof of your car with the palms downwards.'

There was pressure, steady but insistent, between his shoulder blades, until he felt his cheek pressed hard against the icy metal of his car. He felt his teeth chatter as he said, 'My wallet's in my side pocket. You can have whatever money I've got. Just don't beat me up, there's no point!'

But he knew as he spoke that this wasn't a mugging. It was not as bad as that, and yet much worse. He wasn't going to be hit, wasn't going to have his face pulped, his bones broken. But this wasn't going to be the end of it. This was the beginning of something worse than a beating.

The voice said, 'We don't want your money, sunshine. But thanks for inviting us to search your pockets.'

It was the first time he knew that there were two of them. And they did not conceal their satisfaction when they turned out the heroin, cocaine, and Ecstasy. He should never have brought them here. He should have kept to the usual points of supply. It was that bugger Price, pressurizing him to increase his turnover. And he couldn't even shop him, when he was taken in.

He scarcely heard the words of arrest. Despite the steel of the handcuffs pinioning his wrists, it still felt like a bad dream as he rode in the police car to the station.

It wasn't very late – only just past eleven – but it might have been the middle of the night. There seemed to be no one abroad on these minor roads on this autumn Sunday night. Jane Logan was glad of that.

It was safer at night than during the day on these narrow lanes, for headlights gave advance warning of any approaching vehicle. But after she had passed a couple of cyclists in the last environs of Cheltenham, the widow of the late headmaster drove for several miles without seeing another soul. It suited her that way. The thing in the plastic bag beneath her seat was not meant for strangers' eyes.

Her undipped headlamps caught the occasional flash of a familiar name on the old signposts: Deerhurst Walton, Lower Apperley, Bishop's Norton. She remembered the names from happier times in this ancient part of England. She could have used the River Chelt for her purposes, but she drove on towards the wider and deeper waters of the Severn, feeling obscurely that the country's longest river would afford her greater security.

She knew where she wanted to go, but it seemed to take her a long time to reach the old stone bridge with its triple arches. The parking bay was deserted, as she had known it must be at this hour. Earlier on this glorious autumn day, people would no doubt have parked here to walk by the river, glorying in the wide sweep of the Severn's bends beneath the majestic trees, with their first, full-leaved swathes of autumn colour.

She could hear those leaves rustling softly as she slid cautiously from the car. There was a bright crescent of moon now, as there had not been earlier in the evening for the man in black, and stars diamond-sharp against the navy sky. She could just hear the soft surge of the river beneath her from the topmost point of the bridge, and the white, pure light of the moon picked up the occasional ripple where stones were near the surface fifty yards lower down its course.

But beneath the shadow of the topmost part of the bridge, the river at its centre ran wide, invisible and deep. Jane Logan carried the plastic bag carefully, as if she feared that contact with its contents might in some way sully her. She paused for a moment by the keystone of the parapet, feeling her heart pounding, nerving herself for the simple act of disposal.

Then she took the bottom corners of the bag between firm fingers and upended it vigorously over the waters. Time appeared to elongate itself, so that it seemed to her several seconds before she heard the soft splash from far beneath her. She forced herself back to the car on legs which were suddenly reluctant to propel her. But she had to sit for a moment or two with her eyes shut, listening to the gradual slowing of her heartbeat, before she could turn the key in the ignition.

It was as quiet on her way home as it had been on the outward journey. She was into the outskirts of Cheltenham before she saw her first car, and there was only one light left on in her suburban avenue as she drove quietly along it and put the car into the garage.

It was almost midnight, but Jane Logan did not hesitate to pick up the phone. And the tone came only twice before the receiver was snatched up at the other end of the line. 'It's gone!' was all she said.

Nineteen

Tamsin Phillips found that the CID men were waiting for her after morning assembly at Greenwood Comprehensive School. She felt an electric shock of fear when she was told that the tall superintendent and his dozy side-kick wanted to speak to her again, but she controlled it.

She didn't think she showed her emotions to the School Secretary when that middle-aged matron brought her the news. She knew that she must appear perfectly composed when she met the CID. She went quickly into the cloakroom and checked her appearance. She was reassured by what she saw. The short black hair was as neat around the oval face as she had known it would be. She examined the minimal make-up around the large dark eyes. They had always been her best feature, those eyes. They were framed for more exciting things than deceiving policemen, but they might have to work for that, if it came to the pinch.

By the time she strode into the room where they were waiting for her, she was confident about the picture she presented. They had been given Peter's old room for the interview. She'd seen some action, here. But she took care to look around curiously at her surroundings, as though the room was quite new to her. Excitement was good for her, she told herself. Hadn't she always thrived upon it? Couldn't she handle excitement better than anyone else she knew?

'I should be teaching now. There's someone losing a free period to stand in for me, and children aren't being taught properly.' She had produced aggression without making any conscious decision to use it. A good sign, that: it meant she was carrying the fight to the enemy.

Lambert studied her for a moment with his head a little on one side, for all the world as if she had been a naughty child in a tantrum. It seemed a long time before he responded, and she began to feel uncomfortable. Eventually he said, 'It's a pity about that. But even education must sometimes take a second seat to murder.'

It sounded in that moment as if he was accusing her, and her words poured out like an angry denial. 'I told you everything I had to tell last Thursday. This is a waste of time, for both of us.'

'I think not.'

'I was perfectly frank about my affair with Peter Logan. I came out and told you everything. Voluntarily.'

Lambert actually smiled into her flushed face. She found herself wanting to strike him. The smug bastard! She clenched her fists against her thighs as she sat on the upright chair, forced herself to listen carefully as he pointed out quietly, 'Ms Phillips, your initial statement to our officer was full of lies. You told us about your relationship with a murder victim only after we had received information about the affair from a third party.'

'Darcy Simpson! You put more faith in the tales told by that sad weirdo than in what I had to tell you. I told you, I could have him for stalking, if I could be bothered to report the creepy sod!'

'Perhaps. Nevertheless, we had to check out information brought to us by a member of the public. Until Mr Simpson made his statement, you were withholding information in a murder investigation. Made you a lady of exceptional interest to us, that did, Ms Phillips.'

He was using the title she had told him irritated her on Thursday. Was he trying deliberately to rile her? But he must have spoken to dozens of people since then, so perhaps he'd simply forgotten. She mustn't become paranoid. Must behave here as if she'd nothing to hide. She wrinkled her retroussé nose a little, the movement which Peter had said always made him want to reach out and touch her. 'I don't like "Ms". It's ugly, in speech. If we can't have Tamsin, I'd prefer Miss Phillips.'

He nodded, taking away from what she had thought was a tiny victory with his patient smile. 'When we saw you on Thursday and confronted you with what Mr Simpson had told us, you admitted to a serious affair with Mr Logan. Do you now wish to revise anything you told us on Thursday?'

He was treating her as a liar, picking his way around her with a careful choice of words and a tone of voice which might have come from a hostile lawyer in court. He had the air of a man who knows everything, who would be delighted if she now enmeshed herself in his net with further denials. But he couldn't know everything, could he? She said, 'I've nothing to add to what I've already told you. And I would remind you that I'm here of my own volition, helping police voluntarily with their enquiries.'

There was a tautology there, born of her tension, which she was trying hard not to show. She looked from the superintendent's grey, unblinking eyes to the heavy features of that lumpish sergeant, and gave the man the most sudden and dazzling of her smiles. She was shocked when Hook said, 'I should warn you that withholding or distorting information would be most unwise, Miss Phillips. Perhaps you should take a moment to consider your position.' He flicked his notebook to a new page and held his ball-pen at the ready, as if he expected much to be written before they left this quiet room.

Tamsin determined not to show how shaken she felt. She gazed for a moment at the ceiling, suddenly reluctant to use her wide black eyes on these men who seemed so impervious to their charms. She then looked not at them but over their heads as she said, 'I told you last Thursday that Peter Logan and I were having a serious relationship at the time of his death. I told you when I'd last seen him and in what circumstances. I've nothing to add to that. That's not because I'm concealing anything. It's because there *is* nothing to add.'

There was a pause, which stretched until she could bear it no longer, and had to transfer her gaze back to Lambert's face. He was watching her as closely as ever, and when he saw the movement of her dark eyes he said quietly, 'You didn't tell us that your affair with Mr Logan was over several days before his death.'

She wanted to fly at him, to tear his face open with the nails she now felt digging into her thighs as she strove for control. He was bringing it all back, those last, outraged exchanges after Peter had ditched her, the way she had flown at him in her flat, the way he had held her arms above her head so that they should not touch him as she yelled her fury into his face. She could almost feel his strong hands upon her wrists now, almost hear the obscenities she had spat point-blank at the wide mouth she had felt upon hers so often.

'It wasn't over.' The words were so low that she scarcely heard them herself.

She looked up to check if Lambert had heard, found him raising his eyebrows as he said, 'But hadn't Mr Logan set his sights upon someone else?'

'Liza Allen, you mean? That wouldn't have lasted. She was just a young tart who flashed her legs at Peter. I'd have had him back. I wasn't going to let him go off with that little bitch, was I?'

'I don't know, Miss Phillips. Tell me exactly what you planned to do when you found that Miss Allen had supplanted you in your lover's attentions, please.'

She was furious with his old-fashioned phrases, with the way he was probing her about this. Taunting her with it, wasn't he? Throwing that flashy young bitch's triumph in her face and enjoying it. 'It wouldn't have lasted. She opened her legs and gave him an easy shag, that's all. He could never resist that, Peter. But I'd have had him back! He'd have bloody soon come back to me or I'd have—' She stopped suddenly and belatedly, aghast at herself.

'Or you'd have what? Killed him for attempting to leave you?'

She almost rose from the chair in her anger. She wanted to fling herself upon him, upon either of these smug men, to release the anger she felt surging against the frail dam of her throat.

She fought for the control she had been so confident she possessed when she came into this room, but found herself still panting for breath. She caught a glimpse of the photograph of Peter with his wife and family, still on his desk where he had always kept it. They had laughed at the farce of that conventional picture together, but now the faces of his family seemed to be looking up and mocking her, claiming the last laugh after all on her pretensions.

It took Tamsin a long time to retrieve a measure of control. She said in a low, even voice, 'Of course I don't mean that I killed him! It's ridiculous and melodramatic of you even to suggest it.'

'Perhaps. But you have a history, Miss Phillips. Five years ago, you very nearly killed another man because he decided to finish an affair with you.'

She felt the hopelessness of her position. She could hear the despair in her own voice as she stared at Peter's desk and made the ritual denials. 'That was different. And if it had been as you say it was, I'd have gone to prison, wouldn't I? But the matter never came to court.'

'Because Mr Simpson refused to bring charges or appear as a witness. There was no other reason. This time we shall call him, if we need him.'

The wide black eyes which had brought her so many conquests were her enemies now, revealing her fear. She looked up into Lambert's calm, lined face, which seemed to her not to have changed its expression since they began. 'What do you mean? What can bloody Darcy Simpson possibly have to say now?'

'He will testify, if called upon to do so, that you have threatened him with a firearm. A pistol very similar to the one which was used to murder Peter Logan.'

'What?' She heard a peal of laughter, mounting towards hysteria. It took her a moment to realize that it was coming from herself. 'Darcy told you I'd threatened him, did he? Did he also tell you that he was making my life a misery with the way he followed me about? That the very fabric of my new life in Cheltenham was being threatened by this clown from the past?'

'Do you deny that six months ago you threatened him with a firearm? That you told him that you would use it upon him, if he continued to track your movements?'

It was falling into place like a malevolent jigsaw. And she couldn't see what she could do to destroy the picture they were assembling. She tried to work up some spirit, to convey her feeling of mad farce running out of control. But her voice was flat and unconvincing as she said, 'That's ridiculous. Darcy Simpson was never in any danger from me.'

'Do you deny that you threatened him with a firearm?'

'It was harmless. A replica. I waved it at him to try to stop him following me about.'

Lambert waited for her to look at him again before he said, 'You can't expect us simply to believe that, after the string of lies and half-truths you've given us so far.'

'It's the truth. I don't care whether you believe it or not.'

'Then you should care. Your position is now very serious. However, there is an easy way to resolve this matter. You can produce this replica pistol. It won't prove that it was what you used when you threatened Mr Simpson, of course, but it would at least support your story.'

She could hear the scepticism in his every phrase, sense how he saw her wriggling hopelessly in the face of the facts. She looked down, caught the photograph of Peter and his family again in her gaze. Jane Logan's smile seemed to be mocking her now: the wife triumphant at the last over the mistress.

Tamsin said dully, 'I haven't got it. I threw it away.'

'When was this?'

'I don't know. Months ago.'

'A very convenient disposal.'

'Except that it wasn't. If I had it now, I could show you how harmless it was.'

'Maybe. Mr Simpson didn't think it was harmless. According to him, it had the desired effect. He stopped stalking you.'

She summoned up a smile, though she could not imbue it with the contempt she wanted. 'Darcy knows nothing about firearms, Superintendent. He was very easily frightened.'

'Not surprisingly, as you'd almost killed him with a knife on a previous occasion. Did you know where Mr Logan was going to be on the Monday night when he was killed?'

'No. How could I? You know now that he wasn't seeing me any more.' It was the first time that she had admitted that Peter's rejection was final, even to herself, and it shook her more than she could have forecast.

Lambert's calm tones were inexorable. 'You knew that Peter Logan was seeing Liza Allen, didn't you?'

She nodded, near to tears and despising herself for it.

'And you know where she lives?'

Her first impulse was to deny it, but they had exposed her in so much that it seemed futile. She said softly, 'Yes, I knew. I'd taken care to find out. Women like to torture themselves in these situations, you see.'

'And you knew that Mr Logan was at a conference in Birmingham on that Monday?'

'Yes. Everyone in the school did. It had been announced in the staff meeting. It was a feather in the cap of the school that he was speaking as an expert on secondary education.'

'And you had conducted a liaison with Mr Logan yourself

163

over several months. You would know his habits. Didn't it occur to you that he might take advantage of his day's absence from Cheltenham to visit his new lover before he went home in the evening?'

She wanted to deny it, strove hard to summon up the words to do so. But it was so exactly the pattern that their own affair had followed, so much Peter's habit to snatch time like this after a day away, that argument seemed futile. She would have been naive not to see the possibilities Lambert was suggesting, and naivety was not her thing. She said, 'So I knew he might visit his little tart on that Monday evening. So what? It doesn't mean I waited for him near that park in Leckhampton and killed him.'

'It means that you had the opportunity. You gave us a motive yourself a few minutes ago.'

She sought desperately for a reply. 'You can search my flat. You won't find any pistol there.'

Lambert gave her a faint smile. 'You would be very foolish if you kept a murder weapon at your residence. But we may need to search your flat, in due course. For the present, you can get back to teaching history to those children you were so worried about.'

Tamsin Phillips sat alone in Peter's room for minutes after they had gone, scarcely believing that they had not arrested her. Then she went across to the big desk and picked up the outside phone. The voice from the solicitor's office was reassuringly mundane when it asked what she wanted. Tamsin tried to echo its calmness as she said, 'I think I may need legal advice and representation.'

'It's high-profile, John, as we all knew it would be, this Logan murder.' Douglas Gibson stood and poured a cup of coffee for his senior superintendent, treating him like one of the local dignitaries with whom he seemed nowadays to spend so much of his time. Well, John Lambert would be a civilian himself soon enough now, unless the anonymous powers that be above them relented on their decision to retire him.

'Yes, sir. I'm grateful to you for keeping the media out of my hair in the last week.' Lambert resisted the urge to enquire whether there was any news on his own situation. Much better to accept that he was going, that this would be his final case. He was here to report on the state of progress in his last murder case, and that is what he would do.

'I haven't got an arrest for you, or even a prime suspect, as yet. But we've narrowed down the options.'

Gibson grinned. 'You should be dealing with the media yourself, John. Does "narrowed down the options" mean anything or nothing?'

Lambert smiled apologetically: he had been searching for a phrase which would convey how hard his team had been working on the boring necessities of elimination. 'I'll think aloud for you, as I certainly wouldn't like to do at this stage for any media man. There are five major possibilities, in my mind. That doesn't mean our killer couldn't come from somewhere else, but I should now be surprised if he or she did.'

Gibson smiled his encouragement. The nature of his post meant that he was constantly receiving verbal reports on progress; John Lambert had a more lucid and ordered way of presenting things than most.

Lambert, for his part, was wondering how Gibson always managed to look as if his uniform had come straight from the cleaners, with the creases immaculate and the braid with a new-minted shine. The man must be the right shape, he thought without resentment; clothes never seemed to sit easily on Lambert's tall frame.

He said, 'Let's start with the wife, Jane Logan, because we haven't been able to eliminate her. She has a serious relationship going with a man who used to be Chairman of the Governors at Greenwood School. She concealed that from us at first. She says she's planning to marry the man. She also says that Peter Logan would have opposed the relationship and refused to divorce her.'

'Was Logan outraged by her affair?'

'Not according to her. She doesn't think he even knew about it. According to her, he was far too busy getting *his* leg over wherever he could.'

Gibson sighed. He was far too experienced to be shocked by a worthy head teacher's private life, but sex always made for complications, threw too many people into the mix during a murder investigation. He said, 'And what about the other party – this man who was Chairman of the Governors?'

'Steve Fenton. Estranged from his wife; in the process of a messy divorce; anxious not to lose touch with his children. A crack shot, in the past. Didn't need to be that to kill Logan of course, because he was shot at point-blank range. But he did have a pistol, which he claims to have given up years ago, after the Hungerford killings and the tightening of the firearm laws. He certainly hasn't had a licence for the last few years, but there's no record of his pistol being handed in.'

'So either of them could have killed Logan?'

'Either or both. They're alibi-ing each other for the night in question. Claim they were in bed together for most of it. So naturally, no one to confirm their story. Incidentally, we had to prise all this out of them. They were keeping schtum about any liaison until they were forced to admit it.'

Gibson nodded. He was too old a hand to ask Lambert to speculate about what sort of people these two were. The CC was confining himself to the facts of motive and opportunity. 'You said Logan had an eye for the women himself. No doubt that raises other possibilities.'

'We've thrown up two. The latest girlfriend is a Liza Allen. Logan had taken up with her only a week before he died. She had the best opportunity of all: Logan was on his way to her house on the night he died. She knew just when he would be coming and where he would park. He'd rung her to confirm the arrangements only a few hours before he died.'

'Motive?'

Lambert shook his head. 'None that we've been able to establish so far. She's young, attractive and I should think completely bowled over that a man as powerful as Logan in the school should even take notice of her. She's a lab assistant, not a teacher. As I say, he'd only taken up with her a week or so before his death, so it seems unlikely that he was already planning to ditch her. And she came forward voluntarily with her evidence.'

'She sounds like one of a string of opportunities. What about women scorned?'

'Not women. Woman. We've unearthed a few previous conquests of Logan's, but we're satisfied that it's only the last one to be ditched who's a possibility for murder. Tamsin Phillips: thirty-three years old, single, teaches History and Business Studies at Greenwood School. She'd been conducting an intense affair with Logan over the past seven months. Found he was dumping her only days before he died. A fact that she concealed completely from us at first.'

'And obviously she had the opportunity.'

'Yes. And there's more. Tamsin Phillips has a history of GBH. Not a criminal record, because it never came to court. But she was jettisoned by a previous boyfriend, five years ago, and attacked him with a knife. She was rather lucky she didn't kill him, by all accounts.'

'Then why no court case?'

'The boyfriend in question refused to cooperate with the Thames Valley Police. No key witness, no case. Despite the fact that it was he who broke up the affair originally, he's still smitten with Ms Phillips, who I have to say remains quite a dish. He's been following her around for years. Making a nuisance of himself, she says. Which is why she threatened him with a revolver six months ago.'

Even grizzled and experienced Douglas Gibson grinned at the melodrama of it. 'So you've relieved her of the weapon and are making plans for an arrest.' But he knew they couldn't be at that stage. Tamsin Phillips would have been under lock and key now, if it had been as straight-forward as that.

Lambert gave a wry, answering smile. 'She claims that it was a toy replica which wouldn't have hurt anyone. A claim we can't check out, since she says she threw the offending object away some time ago.'

Gibson added the name of Tamsin Phillips to those of Jane Logan and Steve Fenton on the pad in front of him. 'That's three possibilities. Four if you include this Liza Allen, but you obviously don't rate her.'

'Not unless we find anything else to implicate her, no. But there are two other possibilities. The first is our old bugbear, drugs. The Drugs Squad tell me there is a trade around the school, as you would expect nowadays. It's no bigger than you would anticipate in a school of that size, with a sixth form which gets bigger every year, but a source of considerable profit, nonetheless. And there are kids from the school who are dealing in the clubs in Cheltenham: one was picked up yesterday.'

'What's the connection with Logan?'

'There may not be one. Despite his private life, he was an energetic and conscientious headmaster. We've heard from several sources that he knew everything that went on in and around his school. No one knows everything, of course, but we have now learned enough about Logan to believe he knew more than most. I think he knew something about the drug pushers, perhaps far more than was good for him.'

'But is there any evidence of this?'

'Precious little, I'm afraid. But I wouldn't expect much to have been committed to paper. You know what parents think about drugs in schools, and what the press would make of any revelations. Logan was jealous of the reputation of his school; apart from any more unselfish considerations, his whole career was built on it.'

'So you think he knew more than he was telling about drug trafficking as it affected Greenwood?'

'I'm pretty sure he did. The question is, had he discovered enough to put his own life in danger? Not many people appreciate how dangerous a little knowledge of criminal activity can be, when it relates to drugs.'

Gibson shook his head glumly. 'You may well be right. But if this was a drugs killing, we'll probably never pin it on anyone. It would probably be a contract killer.'

'I know. We're following it up, with a view to getting as much evidence as we can before we make any move. There's a local businessman involved, a man using a legitimate firm to cover his drugs activity. We're liaising with the Drugs Squad so as not to put any of their undercover officers in danger.'

Gibson nodded gloomily. 'Let's hope this killing isn't drugs-related, for the sake of our clear-up statistics. I wouldn't like you to finish on a blank, John.'

Lambert noted the first reference to his impending retirement, but thrust it from his mind. 'There's another possibility, sir. Different, but equally unsavoury. A paedophile ring. Logan had contacted the National Paedophile Unit to arrange an interview with them because he had suspicions about a member of his staff. Possibly he was killed to prevent that meeting taking place.'

'So he never named the man in question.'

'No. But we're pretty certain we've found him. Martin Sheene. Teaches science at the school. Logan caught him taking children into the junior science lab during the lunch hour. He denies he's a member of a paedophile ring, but I think he's lying.'

'So what's been done about him? We can't have him near children, if his headmaster thought he was dangerous.' For a moment, lurid headlines danced before the Chief Constable's vision.

'He's been suspended by the school. I've put him under twenty-four hour surveillance. Expensive, but I still have a

feeling that he might lead us to a ring. The National Paedophile Unit is pretty certain there is one in the Cheltenham
area, but they don't know where it meets.'

'It's a week tonight since Logan was killed, isn't it?'

Lambert gave a sour grin. They were both well aware of
the statistic which shouts that if a murder isn't solved in the
first week it's unlikely to be solved at all. 'I'm still hopeful
that I won't end on a blank, sir.'

Douglas Gibson sat back a little in his chair behind the
desk. 'And I'm still hopeful that this won't be your last
serious case, John. I've sent off a lengthy letter to support
my contention that you should be a special case when it comes
to retirement cut-off dates.'

Lambert found himself for once too embarrassed to look
his man straight in the face. He stared out over the bright
orange of the Gloucestershire autumn leaves from Gibson's
window. 'Thank you, sir. I doubt they'll even look seriously
at your letter, though. Bureaucracy can't make exceptions
without bringing in a welter of other requests.'

Gibson recognized a man refusing to allow himself to hope.
'You may be right, John. But I wanted for my own satisfaction
to know that I'd done everything possible to keep you.' He
grinned. 'My letter convinced *me*, at any rate. It made you a
national treasure we couldn't afford to retire.'

'Thank you, sir. Perhaps the National Trust will adopt me.
I'll soon have plenty of time to visit their houses.' He took
his leave awkwardly. He had never requested favours, and
he was uncertain how to respond to them when they were
visited upon him like this.

When he was left alone, the Chief Constable stood looking
out of the same window that John Lambert had stared through.
He realized in that moment quite how much he would miss his
senior CID man. Douglas Gibson hadn't many more years to
do himself now. He felt himself surrounded by young, eager
officers, male and female, who had been recruited into a
police force very different from the one he had entered as

a raw constable in the sixties. John Lambert was a link with those years, able to pit his brains and his methods against the very best of the young officers, yet instantly aware of those very different times when he and the young Gibson had set out on this odd journey through crime.

The world of autumn colour on which the CC gazed took on a sudden shaft of impending winter.

Twenty

M artin Sheene was depressed to the point of desperation. Apart from a half-hour visit to the supermarket to pick up food supplies, he had been sitting alone in his house for over two days now, ever since that grim superintendent and his sergeant had come here on Saturday.

There had been the expected phone call from Greenwood School early on this Monday morning, telling him not to come in, informing him that he was suspended on full pay until further notice. He had made a feeble attempt to contest that decision; it had come to nothing because it was just a secretary at the other end of the line, conveying the bald news of his suspension, blankly refusing to argue because she did not even know the reason for it.

Martin became increasingly restless as the day wore on, thinking of the classes he should have been teaching, of the way the children would be suffering because he was not available. They wouldn't be getting any instruction from anyone else; there were so few science teachers around that there would be no one available who felt competent to take on his classes. He was a good teacher, he thought, especially with the younger children. It would be a shame if they suffered because of his absence.

It was a great pity about his little weakness: it got in the way of all the good work he could do.

And what about the other teachers at Greenwood? What would they be thinking about him? Would they have been fobbed off with some story that he was ill, or would they know that he was suspended? He could imagine the gossip flying around the staff room at lunchtime if they knew that. He had no means of finding out just how much the other teachers had been told. Well, he hadn't many real friends among them, anyway. Just as well, really: he wouldn't be going back to Greenwood now.

He got more and more depressed as the day went on. There didn't seem to be any way out of this. Even if the police didn't pin this killing on him, he wouldn't be allowed to teach again, wouldn't be allowed to do the one thing in life he could do well. He hadn't comprehended that at first, but the knowledge surged in upon him as his lonely Monday dragged on.

It was a grey day to match his mood, with low clouds skidding across the sky on a chill autumn wind. Twilight came early, reminding Martin and the world that the rawness of winter would not be long delayed. He spent long periods watching the leaves swirling past his window; by the end of the day, the chestnut which was the only mature tree he could see had been stripped of its orange autumn cloak and stood like a gaunt skeleton against the darkening sky.

By seven o'clock in the evening, Martin had his anorak on and his gloves ready on the table beside him. There was a meeting of the group tonight. They'd told him not to come, explained that it was safer for him as well as the rest of them if he lay low, in view of the visit he had had on Saturday from the police.

He had spoken to two of them on the phone, and they had both told him the same thing. Keep quiet. Wait for things to blow over. The National Paedophile Unit can't have any real evidence about us, or they'd have moved in by now. But we'd better keep a low profile, all of us. And especially you.

It made sense. Except that they didn't know, couldn't know, quite how miserable he was feeling. How he needed someone to talk to, someone who would appreciate just how depressed he felt at present. If he stayed looking at these four walls much longer, desolation would deepen into despair, and despair into a desperation which might make him do something he would not even put into words.

At seven thirty, as the first notes of the *Coronation Street* music wailed from the television he had long since ceased to watch, Martin Sheene zipped up his anorak, pulled the hood of the garment up over his forehead and ears, put on his gloves, and went out into the night.

Somewhere deep within him, he knew that the group were not his real friends, that they would look out for themselves and throw him overboard without a second thought, if it came to saving their own skins. There were some powerful people among them; he had been surprised at the positions many of them occupied. All they really had in common with each other was a common weakness, Martin thought bleakly. A common sin, if you liked. If you looked at it the way other people did.

It was cold and blustery, without a star to be seen in the black sky in the intervals between the widely spaced street lights. It was a couple of miles to the house, but the walk would do him good; perhaps he could dissipate some of the gloom he felt in the effort of physical activity.

Martin, more determined than ever not to be recognized, pulled his head into the hood of his anorak, like a tortoise shutting out a hostile world. Then, with his gloved hands thrust as deeply as he could into the shallow pockets, he set off in a shambling walk towards the meeting.

He looked neither right nor left. In his misery, he did not see the figure which slipped from the car at the end of the street and followed at a safe distance behind him.

The paymaster whom Mark Lindsay had thought of as the man in black had a name, of course. He was David Sullivan. And after twenty-four hours in the cells, he was so thoroughly cowed that the Greenwood sixth-former who had thought him so formidable would scarcely have recognized him.

The Drugs Squad had questioned him for three hours on

Monday morning and left him wrung out like a damp cloth. He had given them the names of Mark Lindsay and the other youngsters he had recruited as pushers in the schools and clubs. By convincing Sullivan that they already knew it, they had almost tricked him into betraying the name of the man immediately above him in the evil chain, Daniel Price. But he had realized just in time that they knew nothing about the chain of command above him, and kept his mouth stubbornly shut. By Monday afternoon, the Drugs Squad interrogators withdrew, seemingly satisfied that they had got everything he knew out of David Sullivan.

An hour later, a uniformed constable brought him an evening meal. He ate about half of it without appetite or enthusiasm. He glanced up as he heard the steel flap in the door slide back; an eye studied him for a moment through the peephole before the metal was slid back into place. What did they think he was going to do, top himself?

He wouldn't do that. At this moment, he preferred not to contemplate exactly what he should do. Get out of the area altogether, perhaps. That might be the safest course of action. When the drug barons knew you'd been rumbled, you were no use to them any more. Worse than that, you might even be an embarrassment to them, if they thought you knew more than you should. You might be expendable. You might be found in a ditch with a bullet through your head.

This was his state of mind when the heavy door was noisily unlocked. He pulled himself upright, sat on the edge of the unyielding bed as a tall man in plain clothes banged down a chair with its back towards him and sat down with his long legs astride it. The man's grey eyes stared steadily, unnervingly at Sullivan, who was dimly aware of the constable taking up his watchful station in the corner of the narrow cell.

When neither of the men spoke over a period of several seconds, David lost his nerve. He said, 'You've had every-thing I know out of me already. I've nothing more to tell.'

John Lambert nodded. 'Maybe. But this isn't about drugs. Not any more. I'm investigating a murder.'

David Sullivan's mind reeled. He hadn't thought the situation could get any worse. He'd vaguely expected that he would be out of here soon, doing what he could to piece together some sort of life. Yet he was too mentally exhausted to feel any great fear. He said woodenly, 'I haven't killed anyone.'

'Peter Logan. Headmaster at Greenwood Comprehensive. A place where you had pushers operating. A place where you were trying to develop your vile business. I'm sure you know he was shot through the head last Monday. It was a typical drugs killing, Mr Sullivan.'

David looked round the narrow, airless cell. There was no tape recorder running, as there had been earlier for the Drugs Squad interrogation. He couldn't work out what that meant. He tried to force defiance into the words as he said, 'I didn't kill the bastard!'

Lambert studied him for a moment, not troubling to conceal his distaste. 'Want a lawyer, do you? This might get nasty, unless you're ready to cooperate.'

David wondered what that meant. Did they still beat people up in the cells to get what they wanted from them? He looked past the lined face in front of him to the impassive features of the uniformed man by the door. He said, 'I heard about that murder, of course I did, but I don't know who killed the poor sod.'

'He knew about what was going on in his school, didn't he? From what we've been told, he was biding his time until he knew a little more about the chain of supply. Then he was going to destroy you and the rest of your nasty crew.'

It sounded very like the truth to David Sullivan. Logan had been on to what was going on outside the school gates as well as inside them. If the buggers above had only listened to him, if that pushy sod Price hadn't insisted on taking risks when they shouldn't have done, he wouldn't be sitting with the hard edge of this bunk numbing his thighs, talking to this calm, relentless man about murder.

Perhaps they had killed Logan, the people above him. It was the kind of thing they would do, if they decided he was getting too close to the operation. He said desperately, 'I don't know who killed Logan.'

Lambert's grim face relaxed into a half-smile. 'You wouldn't, would you? You're too low in the chain to be involved in decisions like that. You don't look to me like a man with the nerve to place a pistol against the back of someone's neck and blow half his head away. On the other hand, if we find you haven't given us your fullest cooperation, we could treat you as an accessory after the fact. Put you away for six or seven years. Protect the public from you for quite a time, Mr Sullivan.'

Sullivan found himself wishing he had more to give. He'd sing all right, sing like a canary all night long, if it would save his skin from a murder rap. But he didn't know anything worth having, not about this murder. All he could think of now was to give them something, anything, which would take the spotlight off him.

He swallowed hard and said, 'I don't know any more. You need Daniel Price, if you want to find out more about this.'

It was almost nine o'clock when Lambert got into the house. 'I'll get you something to eat,' said Christine.

'Just a drink. I grabbed a sandwich earlier. I'm beyond anything alcoholic. Just a big mug of tea.'

It might have been twenty years and more ago, that exchange, she thought, when the young Inspector Lambert had come in late from a case. The only difference is that nowadays he could not conceal the fatigue he felt after a long day.

Christine Lambert felt herself pulled into the words of a ritual they had conducted many times before as she said,

'You shouldn't be working as hard as this, you know. Even on a murder case.'

But this time he did not shrug her objections angrily aside, shouting that she understood nothing of his job and the way it had to be conducted, as he might have done all those years ago. He nodded a little, then protested feebly, 'It's not all work, you know. Bert and I even managed a game of golf, yesterday.' He could scarcely believe it was so recent. In the weariness which he had allowed to descend upon him once he had reached home, the golf might have been a month ago.

'All the same, you're pushing it. You're working like a twenty-five-year-old, and you can't get away with it any more. None of us can. You'll need to ease up a bit, even if this is your last murder.'

'It might not be.' He regretted the words, almost before they were out. He should never have voiced the thought. It wasn't fair to Christine, and it showed a weakness in himself to be even thinking that way.

There was a pause before his wife asked in a carefully neutral voice, 'What makes you say that, John?'

'It doesn't matter. I should never have said it.'

'But you have. So let's have the full story.'

'There isn't a story, really. It's just that when I was bringing the Chief Constable up to date on this Logan case, he told me he'd made a strong plea to keep me on for another couple of years.'

'I see.'

'But there's probably nothing much in it. I'm sure he's written, if he says he has, but you know what these bureaucrats are. I'm not expecting them to make any exceptions, and I don't suppose Douglas Gibson is either, really.'

'No. You're probably right. I don't think you should get your hopes up too high.'

He took a long pull at his tea. 'No. That's just what I thought.'

He hadn't bothered to deny that he was hoping against hope

to be kept on, to be useful for a little longer, she thought. She and John didn't try to deceive each other nowadays, and she supposed that was a good thing. She said quietly, 'Play the percentages, John. Retirement's the likeliest outcome for you, so be prepared for it. Get ready to enjoy it.'

He nodded. It was so much the best advice that he could find nothing to discuss in it. He was peering down at the TV programmes in the newspaper, not wanting to look his wife straight in the eye, in case he made the discussion more earnest than it was. Looking to change the subject, he said, 'I see there's a programme about Monet on at ten fifteen. I think I'll just watch that, to help me to wind down. I won't sleep if I go straight to bed.'

Monet was a great painter, and the programme about the latest exhibition of his work was excellent. Only a Philistine would have fallen so fast asleep in front of the television set. This one woke up with the empty room going cold and a weatherman chattering cheerfully on the screen.

When he woke next, at three o'clock in the queen-sized bed, John Lambert found his sleeping wife's arm tightened protectively around him.

Twenty-One

C atriona Logan was glad to be back at school. It was
   Tuesday morning, over a week now since her father
had been killed, and she was finding that the routine of
school was a help to her. The teachers had treated her with
kid gloves when she had recommenced her studies at the end
of the preceding week, but when she had come in after the
weekend, things had seemed almost back to normal.

As she left the house at quarter past eight, she felt almost
guilty to be so looking forward to school, so relieved to leave
the house. Mum had been wonderful to her this last week,
had understood everything, had encouraged her to take up
the reins of her life as soon as she felt able to grasp them.
As she fastened the gate behind her at the end of the path
from the front door, she looked back and caught a glimpse
of her mother's white face in the doorway. It gave her an
encouraging smile before the door shut and she was released
to the wider world outside.

Catriona was so delighted to be rejoining her friends after
a joyless weekend that she did not notice the car parked at
the end of the road, nor the man immersed in his newspaper
behind the steering wheel. He did not move for two minutes
after she had disappeared. Then he eased the big Rover
quietly forward and turned into the driveway of the house
Peter Logan's daughter had just left.

The front door opened before he reached it; the same white
face which had made Catriona feel guilty greeted the visitor
with an anxious smile.

For a moment, these lovers who had enjoyed every sort of intimacy did not know what to say to each other. Then Steve Fenton took Jane Logan clumsily into his arms and they held each other for a long moment without speaking, each feeling the rhythms of the other body's breathing, each striving for an emotional closeness to match the physical one they felt.

'I can't stay long. I'll have to be at the office by nine or they'll wonder where I've got to,' he said, as they slowly relaxed their holds upon each other.

So his first words were telling her he could not stay. Would it always be like this, when they had thought that Peter's death would usher in an era of bliss? Jane shut her eyes and clung to him hard, not wishing in that moment to look up into his face and catch apprehension in his eyes. When she felt his arms drop to his side, she held on to him for an instant longer before she slowly relinquished her hold.

She could think of nothing to say but what he already knew. 'I got rid of that bloody gun,' she said.

'Pistol,' he corrected her automatically. The years of familiarity with weaponry died hard.

They were bickering like a long-married couple already, she thought wryly. 'Do you want a quick coffee?'

He looked at his watch. 'Better not, I'm running late already. But thanks for getting rid of the Smith and Wesson. It's better that it's not around, in the present circumstances.'

They couldn't even mention the death which should be bringing them together now. It had become 'the present circumstances'. She had never been tongue-tied with Steve before. Now she could not think of anything to say. Eventually, feeling like a nagging wife as the words came out, she said, 'I was glad to see that pistol go. It made me shudder even to touch it.'

He smiled, forcing himself to sit for a minute on a kitchen chair, pretending to have the time he had just told her he could not spare. He was already regretting coming here at this hour, remembering the shame of hiding in the car until her daughter had gone. He took her hand, but found it was a deliberate rather than a spontaneous gesture. He said, 'Have you said anything to the children about us?'

'No. It's too early yet. Peter was a good father to them. They need to get used to the idea that he's gone. Have you told your two?'

'No. We're still arguing over my access to them, for most of the time. It seems best to keep it quiet until that's been agreed.'

They had thought that the death would release them, but they were still being as secretive as ever. She forced herself to sit down opposite him, but found she could not produce a smile for him. Sensing his unease, she was now wishing – as he did – that he had not come here. She could think of nothing to talk about except the subject she had determined they would avoid when she had asked him to call in on his way to work. She could not look at Steve as she said, 'That superintendent still thinks one of us might have done it, you know.'

He nodded, looking not at her but at the table and its uncleared breakfast crockery. 'One or both of us. It's understandable. We tried to deceive them about our affair, after all.'

He hadn't meant it, but it came out as an accusation. He had wanted to be honest about their liaison to the police, whatever else they concealed, arguing that the CID would discover it anyway. Which they had, of course. She said, 'We've just got to keep our nerve and wait for things to move along. Time is on our side.'

He wanted to question what she meant by that, to ask how time could possibly improve things with the police. But he sensed she would not have an answer, that she would take any query as criticism. They had never been careful about what they said to each other before, not since the very early days. He forced a smile as he stood up and leant forward to kiss her forehead, letting his dry lips linger there for a moment to try to transmit his love for her. 'I must be on my way. We'll have plenty of time together, soon enough.'

That should have been a consolation. It was the sentiment they had offered to each other often enough in the past, when they had had to part.

As she watched him drive away, she found herself wondering for the first time whether that future was actually going to happen.

Daniel Price told his secretary not to put through any calls for the next hour. In the privacy of his own office, he paced around, then placed his forehead for a moment against the cool of the wall, trying to make the brain which worked behind it behave normally.

The voice on the phone had been calm and deliberate, the words enunciated carefully in the Herefordshire accent. A detective sergeant from Oldford, it said. They needed to see him urgently. He didn't like that word 'urgently'. Nor did he like the fact that the voice would not tell him what this was about. He would find out soon enough: the rich local tones had suddenly taken on a threatening note in his ear.

The policemen came quickly, long before he had organized his teeming mind to deal with them. A tall superintendent and the sergeant, whose voice he recognized; he asked them to sit down and took up his station behind his desk. The clock on that desk showed half past nine: too early for coffee. He said briskly, 'I hope this won't take very long. I'm anxious to help the police in any way I can, of course, but you will understand that I've a busy schedule and—'

'How long it will take is the least of your worries,' said John Lambert. 'It would be advisable to cancel your schedule for the rest of the day.'

He was looking at his man with unconcealed dislike. Daniel had never met such immediate and open hostility. He was used to business dealings, where you masked animosity in polite phrases and gestures, however false they might seem to you and your opponent. And even when the traffic police stopped you for speeding, they called you 'sir' and told you what would happen with a cold politeness, keeping things deliberately impersonal. But these policemen in their grey suits seemed to have assumed he was guilty before they started and to see no profit in disguising their feelings. He found their hostility more unnerving than he would have thought possible.

Daniel Price went into the only speech he had had the time to rehearse. 'I don't know what it is that you want to question me about. I run a legitimate business here. We supply computer software to a variety of reputable firms. I don't see why I should discuss them with you, but our financial statements and the record of our dealings are in a filing cabinet on the other side of that wall. You are welcome to peruse them for as long as you like and to come back to me with any questions you like to raise. In the meantime, you must understand that I have—'

'Not interested,' interrupted Lambert. 'Price Computer Supplies may be a wholly legitimate business. Probably is, if you've got any sense at all. It's your other activities which interest us.'

'I've no idea what—'

'Illegal drugs. Class A, for the most part.'

'I don't deal drugs. I never have.'

'Possibly not. The charges will be more serious than that. Running a network of dealers. Providing supplies of a variety of illegal drugs. You'll go down for it. The only question is how long you'll be inside.'

'You've got the wrong man. You'll regret this, when I sue. Because I've never in my life—'

'Save the denials for the Drugs Squad, Mr Price. They're the experts. They'll tie you up so neatly that Houdini wouldn't escape. I'm here to investigate something even more serious. The murder of Peter Logan.'

'You can't possibly think I had anything to do with that.'

'Can't I? I'm prepared to listen to your explanations. They'd better be good. If they are, we shall be checking them out. Very carefully. Because I'd rather like to pin a murder charge on a man who lures youngsters into dependence on heroin and cocaine.'

'You can't pin this on me. I didn't kill Logan!' Price could hear the fear in his own voice.

Bert Hook looked up from his notebook, adding his quiet insistence to the anger Lambert had allowed himself. 'You're going to have to convince us of that, Mr Price. We know you run a network of dealers. David Sullivan is already under lock and key. Your other four dealers are probably being arrested at this moment.'

'I don't believe that!' But even as he shouted the hopeless denial, he knew that it was true.

Hook continued as if he hadn't spoken. 'You were too greedy, you see. Pushed your men too hard, too soon. The Drugs Squad officers have been watching them for some time.'

It was true. He'd been greedy, had tried to grow too fast, in an industry where the profits were huge but caution was the watchword. He felt the sour bile rising to the back of his throat, had to fight down the need to be physically sick as his world collapsed about his ears. His voice was very low as he said, 'You can't have me for murder.'

'That remains to be seen.' Lambert was at him again, brisk when Daniel needed the time to gather what remained of his wits. 'Peter Logan knew about what was going on in his school. He was gathering information which could have affected the whole of your operations.'

'He was being a nuisance, that's all.'

'A bigger nuisance by the day.'

It was almost the exact phrase he had used himself, when he had complained to those above him about Logan. To hear the words coming from this opponent with such chilling contempt shook him, convinced him that they knew far more than he had thought until now. Daniel said sullenly, 'Logan was prying into things he should have left alone.'

'So he had to be removed, didn't he?'

He nodded, scarcely believing that he was admitting this, not daring to put it into words.

Lambert's voice was as quiet as his question was deadly. 'Did you kill him yourself, Daniel? Did you place the pistol against the back of his head and blow him out of your life?'

'No!' He yelled out the monosyllable, as if decibels could convince them that he had not done this. 'I never killed him. You can't have me for murder!'

'So who can we have, Daniel? Who killed an innocent man to keep your evil work alive?'

'I don't know! Look, all I did was pass the word upward.'

'What word, Daniel? The word to eliminate Peter Logan?'

He shook his head, looked suddenly round the room as if he was a stranger in his own office. He wanted to convince them he knew nothing about this, that in all probability this wasn't a drugs killing at all, but he could find neither the words nor the manner to convince. He said in a flat monotone, 'I passed the word upwards that Logan was finding out too much, that's all. He was keeping the information to himself until he knew enough to do us serious damage.'

Lambert studied Price in his wretchedness, calculating whether they had really had every scrap of information out of him, concluding reluctantly that he probably knew no more than he was giving them. That was the way with drugs: the barons at the top used ignorance as a tool, keeping those below them as unaware of their thinking as of their actions, operating like Stalin's secret police. It did not pay to know too much about what they planned, and if Price comprehended what was good for him he would not have tried to find out.

He stood over the hapless man for a moment, then said, 'The Drugs Squad officers are waiting outside. They already know quite a lot about your organization. You would be most unwise to hold anything back from them. And if you wish to offer anything in court in the way of mitigating circumstances, you had better give us any assistance you can in discovering the murderer of Peter Logan.'

The office staff of Price Computer Supplies stood awkwardly aside as the two CID men passed through the outer office. They had heard enough of their boss's desperate shouting to know that something was seriously amiss.

Price's secretary peered fearfully round the door of his room. She saw an abject figure with his head in his hands, a man whose prosperous world had fallen about his ears with an apocalyptic crash.

Twenty-Two

The Drugs Squad superintendent was uneasy. He was used to running his own show. He had undercover officers of both sexes operating within the seamy echelons of the drugs industry, and his prime concern was always to safeguard them from discovery. Murder had to be investigated, of course it did, but it was a complication. He had to be sure that following up even the most serious crime of all did not jeopardize the safety of his operatives.

DI Rushton understood all of this, knew that the tight-knit unit of the Drugs Squad enjoyed more autonomy than any other branch of the service. He understood the reasons for that autonomy. But he knew also that he and the rest of John Lambert's team had to discover the killer of Peter Logan.

If this death was drugs-related, that would make their task much more difficult: the illegal drugs industry employed contract killers, and these professionals were the most difficult of all to pin down. You might be certain in your own mind who had killed one of their targets, but you had to unearth the evidence which would convince the Crown Prosecution Service that this was a case worth taking on.

Chris Rushton wished he could see the man he was speaking to. It was difficult to conduct an argument with an officer of higher rank, and even more difficult when you were pitching your arguments into the mouthpiece of a phone rather than operating face to face. He said, 'I think we've had all we're going to get from this man Daniel Price. He's scared and he's singing, but I don't think he's got any more to give us.'

There was a pause. He could almost see the other man nodding. Then the gravelly voice said, 'You could bail him. See what happens when he gets out. They won't like it, if he's been singing, these people. When they find he's given things away, they might want to make an example of him. *Pour encourager les autres.*'

The French phrase, perfectly pronounced, dropped oddly from that harsh voice. Rushton said, 'Use him as a tethered goat to bring out the lion, you mean.'

'If you like. He'd be no loss to society, even if they got him, a man like Daniel Price.'

'You're probably right. But we can't do it, and you know we can't. Putting a man's life in danger to make an arrest. You know the view the law would take of that.'

He had quoted the book, as the other man had known he would. There was a sigh from the other end of the line, then a moment of silence in which the two very different men were united in a silent contempt for the judges who knew so little of the criminal world. Then the superintendent's voice said wearily, 'What do you propose to do about it, then? I want Logan's killer caught as much as you do, but my priority has to be the safety of my officers.'

'They use Minton for their contract killings, don't they?'

'Recently they've used Minton, yes.'

'We could interview him. Put a bit of pressure on him. Ask him about his movements on Monday the twenty-eighth of September. See if he gives anything away.'

Chris thought he caught a snigger at the other end of the line, but he couldn't be sure of that. The deep voice was perfectly even as it said, 'You won't get anything out of Minton. He's a professional. He'll have covered his tracks efficiently enough, if he did it.'

Chris knew it was true, but he was riled by the other man's dismissal. 'You never know what you might turn up. Even if we could eliminate him from the inquiry, it would be a help.'

The old CID excuse for sticking big feet in where you did not want them. But it was an argument to which there was no real answer. The superintendent said reluctantly, 'I suppose it might. But we'd need to be absolutely certain you weren't using any information which might blow the cover of any of my officers.'

Chris Rushton said, 'You'd have that guarantee, of course, sir. I might even undertake to interview Derek Minton myself, if Chief Superintendent Lambert sanctions it.'

He had thrown Lambert in at the end to outrank that sardonic voice from the Drugs Squad. It was not until several hours later, when he was driving up the M5 towards Birmingham, that DI Rushton thought this might not be such a good idea after all.

Steve Fenton drew up chairs for his visitors and positioned them carefully where he wanted them. He felt as though he was moving pawns in a game of chess which was rapidly running against him.

Lambert said, 'I wanted to check that you hadn't thought of anyone who could vouch for your whereabouts on the Monday night when Peter Logan was killed.'

'No. Except for Jane Logan, of course.'

Lambert gave him a thin smile. 'You didn't have any phone calls during the evening?'

'None that I answered, no.'

Hook coughed discreetly. He had not taken his eyes off Fenton since they came into the comfortable office, with its prints of Tewkesbury Abbey and Gloucester Cathedral on the walls, its sepia photographs of a frowning W. G. Grace and a smiling Wally Hammond. He said, 'There is a weapon unaccounted for, Mr Fenton. You admitted to possession of a Smith and Wesson revolver, of the type we are now certain was used in this killing.'

'I don't think I told you the make of pistol. But it *was* a Smith and Wesson, as a matter of fact. I think I did tell you, however, that I haven't had such a weapon for several years now.'

'That is correct, sir.' Hook nodded, as though very contented to see things falling into place. 'You told us you had given the weapon to the Cheltenham Small Arms Club.'

'Yes. I wasn't shooting any more, even at the club. When the regulations were tightened up after those terrible shootings at Hungerford, I thought I'd get rid of it rather than keep paying to renew a licence I didn't need.'

'Yes, sir. That's what needs clearing up, you see. The club has no record of receiving such a gift from you.'

Hook had spoken so quietly, adopted so thoroughly the pose of a man fulfilling a dull routine, that his bombshell left a silence on its heels which seemed the more profound. In the pause which followed his statement, they could hear voices from the rooms outside, a shout from the street beyond them, a sudden burst of laughter from somewhere along a corridor. Eventually Steve Fenton said very quietly, 'You think I used that pistol to kill Peter Logan, don't you?'

'And did you, Mr Fenton?' This was Lambert, as brisk and direct as Hook had been measured.

'No.'

'So where is that weapon now?'

'I don't know. I – I haven't seen it for years. I thought I'd given it to the shooting club.'

A murderer needs to lie better than that, thought Lambert. This man isn't a natural killer. But then not many murders are committed by natural killers. The majority of killings are committed by ordinary people who find themselves in a desperate situation. He said, 'You'll have to give us a better explanation than that. Peter Logan was shot through the back of his head with a Smith and Wesson.'

Fenton shook his head hopelessly. 'I didn't kill him. I haven't seen that pistol for years.'

They probed a little more, received nothing from him, then

left him sitting dejectedly at his desk. He was well aware that they didn't believe him about the pistol.

It is boring work, keeping a man under surveillance. And cold, once it gets into October. DC Cox was glad of the pale autumn sun which shone fitfully on the windscreen of the Rover, warming the little box which was his prison for most of his eight hours of duty.

Martin Sheene wasn't going to go out again, that seemed pretty clear. Not in the daylight hours, anyway. Just his luck that the bloody man should go out last night half an hour after his shift was over. The murder team seemed quite excited by what they'd found when they'd followed him. Not that they bothered to tell DC Cox about their findings, of course: the blokes who hung around all day and did the weary work of surveillance were the last to be told what was going on.

Just when he had slumped into his seat and thrust his hands deep into the pockets of his jacket, there was action. Limited action, but definitely better than nothing. Sheene had a visitor. A man with the collar of his car coat turned up; a man who looked to right and left along the road before he went up to the door of Sheene's place; a man who gave every sign of being up to no good. DC Cox noted the time of his entry as 14.13 precisely.

Martin was glad when the man announced that he was from the group. He didn't need to say which group; a friendly face from people who shared his interests was just what Martin needed.

But when he had taken his caller inside and invited him to sit down, Martin Sheene found that this man was anything but friendly. He ignored the seat suggested, then cut through Martin's nervous remark about the weather and said, 'You shouldn't have come last night. You were told not to come.'

'I know. But I needed the company. Needed someone to talk to. My mind was reeling. I'm suspended from Greenwood

School. I've probably lost the only job I'm any good at. The only one I really want to do. I needed someone who'd—'

'You shouldn't have come. I'm here to tell you that. I'm also here to tell you that you're out. No one wants you there again.'

Martin Sheene could not believe that the group was shutting him out. He felt the last planks of his rickety refuge splintering about his ears. 'Who are you? What authority have you to—?'

'Every authority. I'm employed by the group. Employed among other things to see that little turds like you get the message. You're not wanted, Sheene.'

Martin felt the panic he'd always felt in the face of physical violence, whether real or threatened. He tried hard to assert himself. 'Now look here, you can't just come into my house and—'

'But I have done, haven't I? And unless you cooperate with me, things could get a good deal worse for you, Mister Sheene.'

He lingered contemptuously over the three syllables of the name, hissing the sibilants with a curl of his thin lips, and Martin was suddenly back in the world of the playground bully, fighting against the panic he felt hammering at his temples. He said faintly, 'Who are you?'

The man gave his first smile. It was not a pleasant one. 'Never you mind that, Martin. Just give me the fullest possible answers to my questions, or things could turn quite nasty for you.'

Martin was unable to look into his tormentor's face. He became conscious of the man's hand, clenching and unclenching in a tight black leather glove. 'What – what is it you want to know?'

'What did Logan know, sunshine?' The man's eyes glittered an icy blue; they were within a foot of Martin's.

'He knew about me. He'd caught me taking a couple of boys into the junior science lab, and he said—'

'Said what a naughty lad you were, yes. We know that. And what did you tell him?'

'Nothing.' Martin was suddenly afraid that this wolfish man was going to hit him, hard and repeatedly. He could not take his eyes off that black fist as it clenched and unclenched.

'You told him about the ring, didn't you?'

Martin had never heard it called a ring before. They'd always referred to themselves as a group. 'Ring' seemed somehow much worse. 'He knew about it. Or at least he gave me the impression he knew.' Martin was suddenly aware of how Peter Logan had made bricks with very little straw, how he had pretended he knew much more than he did. By this means he had trapped Martin into admitting more than he ever should have done. 'I – I said there were a group of us, yes. He gave me the impression he knew already, and I only realized later that—'

'You've been a silly man, Martin. A very silly man. You're going the right way to finish up like Logan.'

The visitor was looking hard into Sheene's face. He brought a second black-gloved hand up to join the one which riveted Martin's gaze, and rubbed the two slowly together. They were acquiring a life of their own, those hands, in Martin's sickly imaginings.

He licked his lips and said, 'Peter Logan phoned the National Paedophile Unit about us, you know, after he'd spoken to me.'

'Yes. You didn't do yourself any good with Peter Logan, did you?'

'No.'

'And you didn't do yourself any good with the ring, not when you went grassing on your friends to your head teacher.'

'It wasn't like that. Peter seemed to know all about it already, the way he talked.' Martin felt the flesh on the back of his neck beginning to creep. Was it because of him that Peter Logan had died? Had those fists which curled and uncurled beneath his horrified gaze placed the pistol against the head of a man who knew too much for his own safety?

Those hands now came slowly up towards his face, then held each side of his head in a vice-like grip, forcing him to open his eyes and look into the man's face as he tried to cringe away. 'Last warning, Sheene. You don't go near the ring again. You're out. And when the police come sniffing around, you know nothing. You give them a single name and you're dead meat. Right?'

'Right.'

The fingers and thumbs which were grasping his cheeks and his ears relaxed slowly, as if reluctant to release their hold. Even when the man lowered the hands slowly to his sides, those hard blue eyes still looked into his face, as if fixing its image in their retinas for future use.

As he shut the door behind this sinister visitor, Martin Sheene felt floods of relief coursing upwards to his brain. His head swam. He forced himself to move to a window to make sure that the man was really leaving.

The man who had loomed so large in the low-ceilinged room seemed a normal size as he moved down the path and away from the house. He was not as tall as he had seemed during his threats, a little round-shouldered, and he walked with a slight limp which Martin had not noticed until now. Almost a diminutive figure, in fact. He did not look back towards the house.

But as he shut the garden gate behind him, Martin caught a last glimpse of those hands, strong as steel beneath the thin black leather.

DC Cox recorded the time of the man's departure as 14.24 hours. He relayed this information to Oldford CID, along with his description of Sheene's visitor.

Jane Logan was back at work in the florist's shop she managed so efficiently. The owner was glad to see her calm

195

presence and direction back in place. The two girls who worked in the shop had made some embarrassing mistakes in the week when they had operated without supervision.

It was there, amidst the heady and incongruous scents of roses and chrysanthemums, that Lambert and Hook conducted their last interview with Jane Logan. It was the first time they had seen her wearing make-up, which she had donned to resume her working role. With her blue eyes and blonde hair, her strong features and air of command, she looked here a busy and attractive working woman rather than a grieving widow.

She took them into a small room behind the displays of flowers in the shop; they sat on upright chairs around a scarred wooden table which had seen much service. Lambert said, 'We saw Mr Fenton about half an hour ago. I expect he's spoken to you since then.'

'No. He may have tried to get through, but the line's been occupied. We've four funerals on Thursday and Friday. I've been talking to the bereaved about the floral arrangements.'

It was probably true, Lambert decided: this was an intelligent woman, who'd been caught concealing information from them already. She wasn't going to lie when there was little point in doing so. He said, 'We were talking to Mr Fenton about a Smith and Wesson revolver we know was in his possession. And in particular about the way in which he disposed of it.'

For a brief moment, there was panic in the light blue eyes. Then she said, 'I didn't want it around, that was all. Not once you'd said it was the kind of pistol which had been used to kill Peter.'

'So you disposed of it.' Lambert nodded slowly, seizing avidly upon the morsel she had offered him while giving her the impression that Fenton had already revealed all this.

She nodded, still unaware that she was offering them anything new. 'I said I'd get rid of it for him. It seemed safer that way. I drove out and dumped it in the Severn on Sunday night. I was glad to see it go. I've always hated guns.'

'Why did you dispose of it like that, Mrs Logan?'

'I told you. We'd heard that Peter had been killed with a pistol of that make or something very similar. It didn't seem sensible for you to find it at Steve's house.'

'Indeed. You were anticipating a police search of his residence at some stage, were you?'

She looked hard into the long, lined face. Perhaps she was realizing now that she had given away more than was necessary. 'I don't know the rules about search warrants. For all I know, you were likely to search Steve's house and mine at any moment.'

Without taking his eyes off her face, Lambert allowed himself a faint smile at such naivety. 'Did you kill your husband with that pistol, Mrs Logan?'

'No, of course I didn't.'

'Did Mr Fenton shoot him through the back of the head with that weapon? Is that why you were so anxious to see the last of it?'

'No! I told you, it seemed a silly thing to keep it around, in the circumstances. That was all there was to it.'

'And where did you see fit to dispose of this dangerous and unlicensed weapon?'

'Out beyond Bishop's Norton. On Sunday night. At somewhere around half past eleven.' She piled up the detail; for some reason, it seemed suddenly important to convince them of what she had done.

Lambert studied her for a moment. 'No doubt you could take us to the spot. It may well be necessary to recover that weapon, in due course. Good morning, Mrs Logan.'

They were gone as abruptly as they had arrived. They left Jane Logan wondering for the first time whether Steve Fenton was responsible for the death of her husband.

Twenty-Three

D I Rushton was wishing he'd let the young woman beside him drive the police Mondeo. He could have done with the time to concentrate on exactly how he was going to question a contract killer.

'You won't need to say anything, Pat,' he said, forcing himself to use the first name of the tall girl with the large brown eyes whom he had brought with him from Oldford. 'You're here to learn, as a young DC. This will be useful experience for you.'

DC Pat Ross wondered why Chris Rushton always had to sound so stiff. The other young ones at the station laughed at him for it behind his back, but he always treated people fairly, and he could be an attractive man, if he would just learn to unbend a little. He wasn't that old: early thirties, she'd have said. Just a mature, experienced man, to a twenty-three-year-old like her. She said dutifully, 'Yes, sir. I've never even seen a professional killer before, never mind spoken to one.'

'He won't admit that he kills for a living, you know. He'll probably strike you at first as perfectly normal: it pays them to be as ordinary as possible.'

'Yes, sir, for obvious reasons. I can see that.'

Chris Rushton wondered if this attractive girl was secretly amused by him; he found himself wondering that quite often with girls nowadays. You couldn't explain to them that it shook your confidence when your wife suddenly announced a divorce you'd never foreseen and took herself off with the toddler you'd adored. You weren't allowed to tell girls you hadn't much confidence, away from your work. Well, not until a later, more intimate stage, anyway; and he never seemed to reach that stage.

Chris spent the rest of the journey thinking about his tactics for the interview at the end of it.

Derek Minton carried an air of good-natured derision about him from the first moment of their meeting. He stood in the doorway of the big modern detached house for a few seconds, eyeing first Rushton and then the observant young woman beside him up and down before he invited them into the comfortable interior of his house. He had them sitting on the edge of a sofa before he said, 'CID getting younger, is it? It was old Lambert and his plod of a sergeant who came to see me last time: I must say this is a considerable improvement.'

He took in the curves of DC Ross beneath her sweater, ran his eyes up and down her nyloned legs with a smiling insolence which stayed just short of open lechery. He enjoyed taunting the police, especially when he felt the ground firm beneath his feet.

Chris Rushton said stiffly, 'You must have heard about the death of Peter Logan. He was the head teacher of a big school in Cheltenham.'

'I believe I did hear, yes. Take a professional interest in all violent deaths, you see. As a criminologist, you understand. Pity about this one, I thought. By all accounts, he was a good headmaster. But I expect Mr Logan was prying into things which didn't concern him. Teachers tend to do that, you know. I didn't like it when my teachers did it.'

'Did you kill him, Minton?'

Derek Minton laughed, unhurriedly and quite heartily. 'Of course I didn't! I don't know where you get these ideas from, really I don't.'

'Perhaps your name comes up because we know of at least four people you've killed in the last two years.'

J.M. Gregson

Minton gave them both a broad smile, then addressed his remarks to Pat Ross. 'I suppose I should really take offence when he comes out with these things – probably threaten to sue for libel. I'm sure a lawyer would call this harassment. Must be embarrassing for a nice young girl like you, finding yourself involved in something as squalid as this.'

DI Rushton told himself that he had expected this. Minton was a professional; he would have covered his tracks and was bound to behave as if he didn't care about their accusations. But Chris still felt his assurance draining away in the face of the man's brazen contempt. He said as truculently as he could, 'So where were you on the night of Monday the twenty-eighth of September?'

Minton pursed the lips of his small mouth. 'Eight days ago, that. I'm not sure I can remember, off hand. Is it important?' He flooded his sharp-featured face with innocence.

Rushton was conscious of the pretty young girl beside him. Watch and learn, he'd said. And now she was watching him being made to look ridiculous. Minton could surely not be this confident, this affable, if he'd shot away Logan's head. Chris felt he was playing out his part in a hopeless charade. He mustered all the boldness he could command to say, 'You'd better be able to prove where you were on that night, Minton. Otherwise we might begin to think you were in Cheltenham, with a Smith and Wesson in your hand!'

'Oh dear, dear, Inspector! DC Ross, I want you as my witness that this man has accused me of something I wouldn't dream of doing. But just for the record, and to show how cooperative I am, how anxious to help hard-pressed police personnel with their enquiries, I think I can supply you with some proof of where I was that evening.'

He walked across the big room to a mahogany cabinet in the far corner and took from the top drawer a single sheet of yellow paper. Rushton looked at it dumbly when it was handed to him. It was the programme for a school play, *Unman, Wittering and Zigo*, by Giles Cooper. It was

200

the date of the production, 28th September, which leapt out at the Inspector. He said, 'So this performance was on the night when Peter Logan was murdered. Hardly your scene, I'd have said, a school play.'

Derek Minton shook his head indulgently, then smiled at Pat Ross. 'Shows how little you know about me, that. My nephew was performing in that play, you see. Very good he was, as a matter of fact. I was surprised how much I enjoyed the play. It's about a class of pupils who take a young teacher apart: very amusing.' He tittered a little in fond remembrance.

Rushton said as sternly as he could, 'And you expect us just to take your word for it that you were there? Or is there anyone around who can vouch for your presence at that play on that night?'

Minton pursed his lips again, enjoying the moment, putting off as long as he could the denouement of the scene. 'My sister and brother-in-law and their other two children. And about three hundred other proud parents and relatives, if you should feel the need for them.'

Pat Ross didn't know what to say to DI Rushton as he gripped the wheel and stared grimly at the road ahead on the way back down the M5. They'd gone a full twenty miles before she managed to say, 'Well, you did say from the start that it was a long shot, sir.'

The Chief Constable was not at his most affable. He had a press conference arranged for midday on Wednesday, only twenty hours ahead, and as far as he could see he was going to have little that was new about the murder of Peter Logan to give the media vultures.

An excellent headmaster had now become a saint in the eyes of the tabloids, and his violent death a commentary on the decline of Britain into lawlessness. Nine days after Logan had died, the television and radio people would be hostile in their questioning about the Cheltenham killing, looking for sound-bites which would make Douglas Gibson and his colleagues seem inefficient, uncaring or both. The CC had been hoping he might have been able to shut them up with an arrest, but that was looking increasingly unlikely.

John Lambert was wondering why he had been summoned to the CC's presence. Gibson was not a man given to wasting time, whether his own or other people's, and it was scarcely twenty-four hours since Lambert had given him a full verbal report on the progress of the investigation. He said reluctantly, 'Do you want me there tomorrow for the media briefing?'

'Yes, I think you'd better be there for this one.' Gibson grinned at his Chief Superintendent's discomfiture: he knew how little Lambert appreciated these occasions. 'I know you think you could be better employed elsewhere, John, but this might be an occasion for showing the flag. If I sit beside the man who's been successful in so many murder hunts, those journalists might give us a stay of execution.'

Lambert nodded gloomily. 'I'll be there. You never know, we may have something to report to them by then.'

'You still think this death might be drugs-related?' Gibson was hoping it wasn't, simply because such a killing would reduce the chances of a successful arrest and prosecution.

'DI Rushton has gone up to confront Derek Minton in Solihull this afternoon. I don't reckon he'll get very much out of a contract killer, but Chris thought it was worth a try.' Lambert kept his face resolutely straight: the prospect of the inflexible Rushton confronting Derek Minton was really no laughing matter.

'Nothing else new since yesterday, I suppose?'

'More than you'd think, but nothing conclusive. Logan's widow has confessed to disposing of a pistol which may or may not have been the murder weapon. Our surveillance man has just reported in that Martin Sheene's had a visitor, but I don't know any details yet. I'm about to go off and see Logan's former mistress, Tamsin Phillips, again. She says she's thought of something relevant, but I have my doubts about how reliable she is. She's a highly strung woman with a history of violence: we've still got her in the frame as a possibility for the Logan killing.'

'Then I won't delay you. There is one piece of good news, however. It's the reason that I asked you to come up here, as a matter of fact.' Gibson smiled at the man who had joined a very different police service not long after he had. 'The bureaucrats aren't as inflexible as we feared. They've listened to my pleas and agreed that Chief Superintendent Lambert is a special case. You're to stay on, John, if you're agreeable. For at least another couple of years.'

Gibson allowed himself a big grin. He wasn't used to delivering good news, had found himself in the end anxious to get it over with quickly. He shrugged aside the man's thanks, was touched to see how delighted a grizzled warrior in the fight against crime could be by the extension of his war. 'Don't bother to thank me, John. They've done *me* a favour, as well as you.'

It was only when John Lambert had gone on his way that Douglas Gibson wondered how pleased the man's wife and family would be when they heard the news.

Bert Hook drove carefully through an irregular trail of pupils leaving Greenwood Comprehensive School, whilst Lambert stared through the window and marvelled again at the vast range of emotions on display in the minutes after the end of a school day, from small boys racing along in ecstasy at their release from the classroom to older children trudging with their eyes fixed upon the ground, as if despair could grow no deeper.

Tamsin Phillips was waiting nervously for them in the reception area of the school. She gave them the briefest of greetings before turning briskly upon her heel and leading them down a long corridor and into the History Resources Room, the small room at the back of a classroom where they had conducted their first interview with her.

She was plainly ill at ease, but if anything it improved her dark good looks. Her agitation flushed her face a little beneath the curls of shining black hair, the retroussé nose making her look younger than her thirty-three years and in need of protection. This woman could play the damsel in distress card to great effect, if she should need to, thought Lambert. It was easy to see why that strange, vulnerable, former partner of hers, Darcy Simpson, still felt drawn to her all these years after she had taken a knife to him.

She waited until they were sitting on the hard upright chairs before she said, 'I asked you to come here. I suppose I should take the initiative and tell you why.'

She gave them a winning smile, switching it from one to the other as she sought for a response. She got nothing from Hook and only the curtest of nods from Lambert. They weren't about to make a nervous woman less nervous.

She had anticipated questions, wondered now quite where she should start. She said uncertainly, 'Well, after our last meeting, I took some legal advice from a friend of mine.'

'And he no doubt told you that you should be telling the whole truth. Unless you killed Peter Logan, of course.' Lambert stared evenly into her pretty face.

It was so nearly exactly what her friend had told her that she was thoroughly disconcerted. 'I didn't kill Peter. It's because I want you to get whoever did kill him that I've asked you to come and see me now. However, the legal advice was much as you suggest.'

'I'm sure you were told that you should tell us the truth and hold nothing back. I hope you are planning to do that now. I would remind you that this is our third meeting with you. It is high time that we had the complete story.'

She flushed even more deeply, in a mixture of embarrassment and anger. She had thought the days of being rebuked like a naughty child were long over. But this infuriating man would no doubt tell her that she had behaved like a child. Tamsin Phillips looked fiercely at the dusty table in the middle of the room, as if it were necessary to her concentration. 'You've already had it. Everything I told you yesterday was true.'

'But incomplete. You said you had more information to give when you asked us to come here today.'

'Yes. I didn't realize at the time that it might have been important. It now seems to me that it might be.'

'So let's have it. With nothing held back and no embellishments, please.'

She looked from the stern-faced superintendent to the rounder face at his side, but found no relief in Hook's impassive countenance. 'I told you yesterday that I was aware that Peter was seeing Liza Allen. I think I lost my head a little and called her a little tart. I'm sorry about that.'

'No doubt Ms Allen will survive it.' Lambert was impatient to hear whatever new thing she had to tell them.

'You suggested that I knew Peter's habits. That I would know what he would do after his day at the Birmingham conference. It's true enough: I knew his habits well enough from his months with me. I knew that he would be likely to take advantage of a day's absence from school to visit a lover in the evening before he went home. What I didn't tell you yesterday was that I tried to confront him when he made that visit.'

Lambert tried hard not to show his excitement. 'You had better tell us what happened when you did that.'

She nodded, determined now to complete the tale and rid herself of the burden of concealment. 'I'd have told you yesterday if I'd thought this had any bearing on the case. At the time I couldn't see that it did. Probably it doesn't, but I want you to know the full story.'

'And why didn't you want us to have that yesterday?'

'I wasn't proud of myself and the way it would look. The discarded mistress, waiting around the door of the new one to cause a scene and try to claim her man back. It's not a very edifying scene, is it? Especially for a liberated woman

like Tamsin Phillips!' The self-contempt in the last phrase
seemed almost physically painful for her.

'This is a murder inquiry, Miss Phillips. Let's make sure
we have everything this time. It's the third time of asking.'

'That's the only thing I didn't tell you yesterday. That I
tried to intercept Peter Logan as he went to visit his latest
conquest! I found Liza Allen's address from the school records. I went and parked at the end of her road in Leckhampton
and waited for Peter to arrive. I knew he probably wouldn't
park right outside her door because he was cautious like
that. Careful of his reputation as the divine headmaster!'
She struggled for a moment to control her bitterness.

'What time did you go there?'

She controlled her emotions, then resumed in a lower,
almost matter-of-fact voice. 'Around seven o'clock. I was
there for over an hour, because obviously I didn't know
exactly when he would come. I played CDs in my car; I
didn't want to put the light on to read in case it made me
conspicuous. Eventually I decided that Peter wasn't coming,
after all. So I gave up and drove off. I suppose I took the route
alongside the park because I realized that that was the sort of
quiet place where he'd park. That's when I saw his car.'

'And was there any sign of the driver?'

'No. I got out and looked. There was no sign of Peter.'

'Did you go into the park?'

'No!' She looked both startled and terrified by that suggestion. 'My first thought was that he must have only just
left the car, that he must be on his way to Liza Allen's
flat by a different route than the one I'd driven. So I turned
back and drove quickly round there, hoping to intercept
him at her door. But there was no sign of Peter. I waited
a couple of minutes, then decided that I'd missed him
and he was probably inside the flat with Liza. I drove
back to his car – there still no sign of him, so I
went home.'

It was flat and anticlimactic, not the way a story like this should end. Lambert said, 'Did you see anyone else around his car?'

'No. It's a quiet road and it was deserted.'

'That's a pity. Because it was around this time that—'

'I did the first time, though. The first time I spotted Peter's car.' The large dark eyes were wide with the recollection, full of a desire to convince them that this time at last she was telling the complete truth. 'I saw a man coming out of the park. I think he went to a car further down the road. I couldn't be sure of that, though, because I scarcely noticed him. I was looking for Peter at the time. It's only since I've gone over that night in my mind that I've remembered this man.'

Lambert wondered if that was true, wondered whether this emotional, inconsistent woman was even now providing another diversion for them. He said brusquely, 'Describe this man for us, please.'

'I can't! That's the trouble, you see, I didn't give him any attention at the time. I wasn't looking for anyone except Peter.'

'Was he tall or short? Thickset or slight?'

'I don't know.' She sought desperately for something which would convince them that the man existed at all outside her imagination. 'It was dark and I didn't give him any real attention.' She furrowed her brow, staring not at her interlocutors but at the table. 'He wasn't particularly tall or I'd remember it. I have an impression that he was slight rather than broad.' She suddenly became very animated. 'And I think he was wearing a tracksuit. Yes, I'm sure he was, because I think I presumed at the time that he'd been out jogging. But he wasn't running at the time. I think he just came out of the park and went down the road to his car.'

'Do you recall anything about that car. Large or small? Even the colour might be some help.'

She shook her head in frustration. 'I never even looked at it. I just have the impression that there was another car, fifty

207

yards or so behind Peter's Rover 75. A car which was there the first time I went there and not there at all when I drove past again about five minutes later. I don't even know that this man got into it, but I'm fairly sure the car was gone when I came back to the spot the second time.'

Hook leaned forward, gave her the first smile she had collected from either of them. 'Concentrate, Tamsin. This may be the man who killed Peter Logan. Think very hard. Try to see if even now you can recall some detail about him which might help us.'

He had spoken quietly and earnestly, but by now she had caught some of the excitement of two men whose job was to hunt people down. She screwed up her closed eyes with the effort of her concentration. After a couple of seconds, those dark, expressive circles opened very wide. 'He walked awkwardly, somehow. I think he had a limp. Yes, I'm sure he had! He was going the opposite way along the street to me, but I caught him in my headlamps for a second as I drove past him. He was hurrying along with his head down, and I remember his right shoulder kept dropping as he moved.'

Twenty-Four

Phone-tapping is a sensitive subject. It is an ongoing matter of friction between those who strive to ensure that the law of the land is obeyed and the Civil Liberties lobby. It is right that it should be so, for phone-tapping needs to be sparingly used: it has overtones of the police state.

But some crimes are potentially a greater attack upon liberty than the measures taken to combat them. One of these is paedophilia, which brings a vast range of horrors to those in society who are least able to defend themselves. The full details of the membership of the paedophile ring attended by Martin Sheene became clearer after he had been followed to their meeting place.

There were some high-profile members, including a circuit judge, a high-ranking civil servant from GCHQ in Cheltenham, and the Chief Executive Officer of a large insurance company. Martin had only been admitted because he worked with children; there was an unvoiced thought that he might at some future stage provide them with a new range of the vicious pleasures they sought.

The request for phones to be tapped had to go through several stages, but Douglas Gibson was grim and determined and red tape was mercifully absent. Within less than twenty-four hours, the Chief Constable had obtained his permission from the Home Office and the taps were in place.

The man who had so frightened Martin Sheene was Clive Boby. He made phone contact with the man from GCHQ late on the night of Tuesday, 6th October, seven hours after DC

Cox had reported his exit from Sheene's house. In doing so, he confirmed both his own identity and the position of the man he rang.

Clive Boby was a man who retailed his deadly services to a variety of criminal groups. A professional killer, that most elusive of villains for the police to pin down.

The man he phoned was Geoffrey Lawson, a senior civil servant at GCHQ in Cheltenham. The content of the call confirmed him as both the man who gave Boby his orders and the unofficial secretary of the paedophile group.

Lambert listened to the tape of their conversation twice before nine o'clock the next morning. Then he rang the National Paedophile Unit in London and set in motion a complex police exercise which would climax in the simultaneous arrest of the ten members of the paedophile ring. The operation involved nearly a hundred officers, but the police machine is very efficient in these large-scale swoops: within two hours the various nets were ready to close on the still unsuspecting prey.

Amidst all this, John Lambert was concerned only with the arrest of a murderer, Clive Boby. At three twenty on that Wednesday afternoon, ten minutes before the hour designated for the mass arrests of the paedophile ring, Lambert and Hook drove into a quiet suburb on the northern side of Hereford.

It was a broad road, wide enough to accommodate mature trees on the edge of its pavements. Large nineteen-thirties detached houses stood well back from the road on spacious plots. Most of the trees still held a full clothing of leaves, which had only the beginnings of the autumn colour which would make this such a handsome avenue in November. There was a mature chestnut where he parked, however, which had already turned an opulent orange. The road around it was strewn with its fallen leaves, covering the squashed shells of the nuts which had fallen many weeks ago. Not many children lived round here to gather conkers.

Lambert parked his ageing Vauxhall Senator near this tree,

some thirty yards from the gates of the house he proposed to enter. He made no move until two other unmarked police vehicles drew up quietly behind him.

At precisely three twenty-seven, Lambert and Hook walked up to the door of a big house, which had the thick boughs of a well-established wisteria trained over the porch and climbing roses still blooming bravely against the warm bricks of the front wall. It was a far grander house than either of them could ever have aspired to from the right side of the law.

Lambert gave the bell one short push. Then, after a few seconds with no response, a longer, more insistent one. They could hear only the sound of the bell inside the empty house: it is curious how a house can seem empty, just because the ring of a bell brings no answering response of movement from within. But this house was not empty. There was no sound of footsteps upon its solid floorboards, but the wide oak front door was eventually opened by a wiry man of about thirty-five.

He was in shirtsleeves. Lambert inspected him for a couple of seconds. 'Are you Clive Boby?'

The man nodded, then inspected their warrants unhurriedly and with no visible reaction, though the presence on his doorstep of a detective chief superintendent and a detective sergeant must surely have set his pulses racing. He said, 'I can't think what you want, but you'd better come in. I was in the snooker room, potting a few balls on my own.'

He led them through a dining room which looked as if it were seldom used to an extension behind the house, where thick curtains shut out the bright afternoon and fluorescent lights shone brightly over the variously coloured balls on a full-sized snooker table. He picked up a cue and potted balls as they talked. Bert Hook watched him warily, wondering if he would use the cue as a weapon if he felt cornered.

But Clive Boby was a professional killer, who calculated the odds with a clear mind: if he saw that things were hopeless for him, he probably wouldn't move into desperate, useless action. It seemed now that he just wished to demonstrate the steadiness of his nerve, for his hands remained perfectly still as the conversation proceeded while he addressed and potted a series of reds and colours.

A snooker table is twelve feet long and six feet wide. It needs a large room to accommodate one: a room at least twenty-two feet long and sixteen feet wide, to allow a player to cue properly. Clive Boby was moving considerable distances between some of his shots.

And as he moved, he limped slightly, dropping his right shoulder to accommodate the movement.

Boby potted a long red and kept his head absolutely still for a moment as he watched the cue-ball roll into perfect position on the black. 'I want you to note that I've been cooperative. I can't imagine why you've come here, but I've invited you freely into my house and I shall answer to the best of my ability whatever questions you wish to put to me.'

Lambert watched as the black ball crept towards the pocket and dropped in with its last roll. Then he said quietly, 'How much did you get for killing Peter Logan?'

Boby smiled quietly but didn't look at him. 'Wasn't me, Lambert. There are one or two headmasters I'd like to have shot, years ago, but the Cheltenham one wasn't down to me.'

'We have a warrant to search these premises. I think that among other things we'll find the Smith and Wesson pistol which killed Mr Logan. There are powder burns on what's left of the neck of Peter Logan, and most of the point of entry of the bullet is still intact. I expect the forensic boys will tie up your weapon with the wound: they're very ingenious nowadays.'

A red disappeared precisely into the centre of the middle pocket. Boby said, 'I was elsewhere at the time. You won't tie me up with that one.' Hook thought that his voice seemed minimally less confident, but he couldn't be sure.

Lambert watched his man as he moved round the table.

'We shall see. There was a hair on the shoulder of the body which didn't come from Peter Logan. And a saliva sample from the back of Logan's car coat. We'll have a DNA sample from you, once you're safely under lock and key. I should be surprised if we don't get a match. Clever people, these DNA boys.'

Boby attempted a long blue into the bottom pocket, watched it wriggle in the jaws and stay out, mumbled a low curse. He slammed a red hard into the green pocket, as if he needed that precision to restore his assurance. 'Can't help you on Logan's killing, I'm afraid. Like to be of assistance to the police whenever I can, of course, but what you don't know you can't tell.'

'We don't need a confession, though I expect you'll give us one when it becomes inevitable. We have a tape of your conversation with Geoffrey Lawson last night, you see. That's every bit as good as a confession, in its own way.'

This time Hook was sure there was a reaction from the man. Boby had his back to them, crouching over a pot on the pink, but there was a definite stiffening in his body. He potted the pink all right, but the white he had meant to stop dead shot forward and almost followed the pink into the pocket. Two or three seconds went by before Boby said, 'Don't even know the man. You must have a tape of some other poor sod. Good try, but no cigar today, men! Now go and persecute some other bugger, Lambert!'

'We're in the right place, Boby. The sound boys at forensic will have no difficulty proving it's your voice on that tape.' Lambert looked at his watch, aware that by now he had the attention of the man pretending so studiously to ignore him. 'Geoffrey Lawson's been arrested in the last five minutes: I don't see him keeping quiet to save your skin.'

The cue dropped on to the slate bed of the snooker table with a noise like a pistol shot. Clive Boby stood up and looked at the two men standing on the other side of the table. 'There's no tape to pin me down, Lambert. Even if I'd ever spoken to this man Lawson you spout about, I'd never have given you anything useful.'

Lambert smiled. He had often found himself beset by shafts of sympathy when arresting murderers, who were too often ordinary people caught in extraordinary circumstances. For this man he had not a shred of sympathy. He felt only exultation in the rare arrest of that most elusive of murderers, the contract killer. He said, 'How about, "I told Sheene he'd get what I gave Logan if he opened his mouth about anything"? I don't see a prosecuting counsel letting that go. Of course, by then you'll probably be pleading guilty, I should think.'

He nodded to Hook, who stepped forward and pronounced the formal words of arrest: 'I arrest you on suspicion of the murder of Peter Logan. You do not have to say anything, but it may harm your defence if you do not mention when questioned something which you later rely on in court. Anything you do say will be recorded and may be given in evidence.'

Hook had taken care to get between table and player, so that the snooker cue was no longer available as a weapon. Boby said nothing, but for the first time he had a hunted look, like a cornered animal. Lambert said calmly, 'As well as my own car, there are two police vehicles outside. An Armed Response Unit is covering the rear of this house as well as the front entrance. There is no way out for you.'

Clive Boby eventually moved out to the car in handcuffs, walking between two uniformed policemen with that slight limp which had helped to identify him. He did not look like a man who had killed at least eight men in his career.

Lambert walked slowly round his garden in the soft gold of a still October sunset. He had the familiar flat feeling of anticlimax that he had now come to expect after an arrest and the conclusion of a murder case.

Christine watched the tall, slightly stooping figure through the kitchen window with a mixture of affection and irritation. Her husband sniffed a rose, flicked earwigs from the flowers of dahlias which were still awaiting the doom of the first heavy frost, inspected the buds of the chrysanthemums he would move into the greenhouse at the weekend. He became more relaxed as she watched, moving contentedly from bed to bed, surveying his handiwork, appreciating the ripeness of autumn, planning what he must do during the winter.

John Lambert enjoyed his garden, would protest to visitors that, even with his wife's devoted help, he never had enough time to bring it to perfection. But at this moment, he was full of a silent delight that he would be able to go on making that complaint.